THE KOUFAX DILEMMA

Steven Schnur

ILLUSTRATED BY
Meryl Treatner

AN AUTHORS GUILD BACKINPRINT.COM EDITION

THE KOUFAX DILEMMA

AN AUTHORS GUILD BACKINPRINT.COM EDITION

Published by iUniverse.com, Inc.

For information address:
iUniverse.com, Inc.
5220 S 16th, Ste. 200
Lincoln, NE 68512
www.iuniverse.com

Originally published by Wm. Morrow

ISBN: 0-595-19998-4

Printed in the United States of America

For David
my favorite ball player

anny, you're going to the seder, and that's final," Mom said, her voice rising in sudden annoyance.

"I can't," I told her, punching the pocket of my mitt.

"Don't tell me you can't. It's not up for discussion. Now, I don't want to hear another word." She turned back to the mirror and continued brushing her hair.

I stood by the bedroom door, watching her reflection and planning what to say next. All afternoon I'd thought about it. I knew just how Mom would respond. I didn't expect to convince her right away. But when she realized how important the season opener was—against Ryewood, the only team that had beaten us last year—I knew she'd give in. I just had to stay calm. If I got frustrated and angry, she'd never come around.

"Coach is counting on me," I pleaded. "He even told me I'm starting. I've been pitching really great lately. I worked all winter for this."

"I'm sorry, Danny. But Coach will just have to do without you for one afternoon. We've been over all this before. He should be ashamed of himself for scheduling a twilight game on the first night of Passover. He's Jewish, after all."

"It's not his fault. The league does the scheduling."

"Then the league should be more sensitive. Would they ask you to play on Easter Sunday? There are more than just a handful of Jews in this town."

"Jim Cohen's parents are letting him play."

"That's their affair. You're not going to."

"What's so important about a seder?" I almost said "stupid seder." This wasn't going the way I'd expected.

"If you have to ask that question, you need to pay better attention in religious school."

"I hate religious school."

"You're full of complaints today, aren't you."

She chose a necklace from her jewelry box and held it against her blouse. "The seder is important because freedom is important. Every Passover we remind ourselves how terrible it is to live as slaves and how precious our freedom is. If we forget that, we might lose it."

"Well, couldn't we start the seder a little later, then?"

"The holiday begins at sundown. That's the tradition. Anyway, it's not our seder. Ellen's gone to a lot of trouble. It's gonna be delicious."

"I don't care about the food. I wanna play."

"I know you do. And I wish I could say yes. But I can't. One night a year, Jews all over the world sit down together to remember their history, eat, sing, and celebrate, and we're going to be a part of that."

"Mom!"

"I'm not going to argue with you anymore. You're going, and that's final—end of discussion."

"Come on, Mom!"

"Danny!"

"You're so unfair!"

"It's just not right to play baseball the first night of Passover," she declared, "not if being Jewish means anything to you."

"Then maybe it doesn't," I declared, my voice rising.

"You wouldn't talk that way to your father."

"Dad doesn't care," I snapped. "He and Marie are never around for the holidays. They're always taking trips."

Mom frowned, then began searching through her closet for something. "Helaine will be here any minute," she said, her voice muffled by her clothes. "I want you to eat a good dinner—that means vegetables, too—and no television until you've finished your homework."

"Are you going out with Arthur?"

"Yes, I'm going out with Arthur!" she mimicked. "Did you see my black evening bag?"

I shook my head. "He's such a nerd!"

"What's nerdy about him?" Mom asked, turning toward me.

"Everything," I growled. "All he ever talks about is the stock market. He doesn't know a thing about sports, and he listens to the worst music in the car. And he's old."

"Arthur's not old!" Mom objected. "He's prematurely gray. And just because he doesn't share the interests of an eleven-year-old doesn't make him a nerd."

"Yes, it does."

Ali wandered into the bedroom, holding a

half-empty bottle of juice in one hand and her teddy bear in the other. Mom's small black purse hung around her neck like a security badge.

"No go out, Mommy," she said.

"Just for a little while," Mom told her, removing the purse, then kneeling down to tuck in Ali's shirt.

"Gimme," Ali insisted, reaching for the purse.

"Mommy wants to use it tonight, sweetheart."

"Ali *need* it."

"Helaine's coming to take care of you," Mom said, trying to distract Ali by draping a colorful scarf over her shoulders. "Look how pretty." She turned her toward the mirrored door.

"Want Mommy," Ali declared, ignoring the scarf and grabbing hold of her dress.

"Please, sweetheart, don't get Mommy's clothes messy." The doorbell rang. "That's probably Helaine," she said, emptying her everyday purse onto the bed. She opened the black one and swept her most important things into it. "Coming!" she yelled, running down the stairs.

Ali yanked the empty purse to the floor and stuck her bottle in it, then hung it around her neck. I walked over to the window and looked down at the antique Studebaker parked in front of the house. Helaine's husband, Sol, stood by the driver's side, polishing a spot on the roof. He was always washing and simonizing the car, calling it his "baby." Helaine often complained that he paid more attention to "that heap of chrome" than he did to her. As she entered the house, he waved, eased himself back behind the wheel, and drove slowly out of sight, the huge bumpers gleaming brightly in the late afternoon sunlight.

How come Mom and Dad couldn't stay married forever, like them? I wondered, turning back to the room. Mom's clothes lay scattered over her side of the bed. The other side, where Dad used to sleep, was empty. When I asked Mom once why she still kept his side of the room so neat, she looked around in surprise and said, "I guess the habits of eleven years are hard to break. I still think of it as Daddy's side."

Their wedding picture stood on the dresser. After the divorce, Mom had removed almost every sign of their marriage. Even the picture had disappeared awhile, about the time Dad remarried. In its place she had put a photograph of white-haired Arthur. He looked old enough to be her father. Then one day the wedding portrait returned and Arthur vanished. When I asked Mom about the change, she said, "Your father and I had a good marriage."

"Then why'd you get divorced?"

"We grew apart. It happens. We wanted different things from life. But just because our marriage didn't last doesn't mean we made a mistake. Nothing lasts forever. We loved each other once. We created two beautiful children. We're still your parents, even if we don't live under the same roof."

The doorbell rang again.

"Danny, I'm leaving," Mom called upstairs. Ali followed me out of the bedroom, clutching Mom's purse to her chest.

"Bye," I said sullenly.

"I'll be at the New Moon restaurant if you need me. The number's on the fridge. In bed by ten, please."

Ali dropped to her bottom and bumped slowly down the stairs, then hugged Mom's legs.

"You be a good girl and go to bed when Helaine says."

"Mommy back soon?" Ali asked.

"Soon, sweetheart." She released Ali and blew me a kiss. "Come on, Danny, cheer up. It's only one game. You've got the whole season ahead of you."

I didn't answer; I just glared at her. She put her hands on her hips and glared back, imitating me, took one last look at herself in the mirror, then opened the door.

Arthur stood holding the screen door with one hand, hiding the other behind his back. He wore white pants, a red polo shirt, a blue sports jacket, and Top-Siders. His bushy white hair looked like a snowball.

"Don't you look lovely!" he said to Mom. His hidden hand came forward, holding a large bouquet of yellow tulips.

"How beautiful," Mom said, surprised.

"Happy spring," he declared. Mom took the bouquet and asked him to come in while she put the flowers in a vase.

Arthur released the screen door and stepped inside. "And don't you look beautiful, too, you little doll," he said, kneeling down and taking Ali's face in his hands. I didn't like him calling Ali "little doll," or me "Danny boy." He always tried too hard to be friendly.

"Ali go, too," she said, puffing out her chest to show him the purse.

"Yes, I see," he replied. "You're all ready to go dancing." He reached into his pocket, pulled out a shiny penny, and dropped it in her purse. "Now you're all set." Ali looked down at her chest and smiled.

Arthur rose from the floor, grunting, then turned to me and said, "How ya doin', Danny boy?"

"Lousy," I muttered.

"Lousy? How can you feel lousy on such a beautiful day?"

"Don't ask," Mom called from the kitchen.

"Can I help?" he whispered, opening his eyes wide.

I didn't really want his help, but I wanted to play the opener so badly I was willing to try anything. "Mom says I have to go to Ellen's seder and miss our first game. I'm starting pitcher that night."

"That's a tough one," he admitted, pressing his lips together.

"Don't badger Arthur," Mom said, returning with the flowers in a glass vase and setting them on the table by the stairs. "He can't help you and isn't even going to try, if he's smart." She winked at Arthur. "Shall we?" she asked, taking his arm. "Be good, kids."

"Sorry," Arthur said to me, stepping back outside with Mom.

"Wimp!" I muttered, watching them walk down the path. Arthur was a head taller than Mom. He held the car door for

12

her, then folded himself into the black Porsche—the only cool thing about him— started up the noisy engine, and drove away.

"I'm not missing the opener just to go to some dumb seder with people I don't even like," I declared, closing the door.

"Come on down, Danny, dinner's getting cold," Helaine called from the bottom of the stairs. "What are you doing up there all alone?"

"Nothing," I said, sitting at my desk, staring out the window.

"Then come do *nothing* with your sister and me," she insisted. Helaine was short and round and wore her long gray hair coiled on top of her head. It reminded me of a tarnished silver teapot. "I haven't seen you kids in two weeks. I need some good gossip. How's school? What's cool this week? What's dumb? And what's new with the greatest Jewish southpaw since Sandy Koufax?"

I walked slowly down the stairs and followed her into the kitchen. Helaine often stayed with us on Friday or Saturday evenings and whenever Mom had to work late. She'd been our sitter for as long as I could remember. The few times Mom went away on business, Helaine moved in, bringing along her quilted robe, a flannel nightgown, and pink furry slippers that Ali loved to pat. Her own kids were married and had children of their own.

"What do you think of Arthur?" I asked, dropping into a kitchen chair.

"Hoo-ha! A serious question right off the bat."

"You think Mom's gonna marry him?"

"Has he popped the question?" she asked with sudden interest.

"Want lollipop," Ali demanded from her high chair.

"No candy until you finish your dinner, young lady."

"She never tells me anything," I complained.

"Well, if it's any consolation, she doesn't discuss her personal life with me either." Helaine removed the chicken from the oven. "Wash up."

"Mom and Arthur argue sometimes," I said, standing by the sink.

"That's a good start," Helaine declared, cutting Ali's chicken into small pieces on her ABC plate. "What's marriage without a few good disagreements to get the blood pumping? Sol and I argue all the time. At our age, it's the only exercise we get. I can't stand the way he drives—he complains about my cooking. Every time I get into the car, I tell him to go faster. Every meal he says, 'I'm willing to pay for cooking lessons.' We don't mean anything by it. It's just the way some couples communicate. I love my Solly dearly."

"Mom and Dad never argued," I said.

"Maybe that was their problem. They

should have done a little more yelling instead of keeping it all bottled up. You too. Let your feelings out. You're much too serious." She poked me in the ribs with a wooden spoon.

"Arthur's too old. His kids are in college already."

"If he's old with college kids, what am I with three grandchildren?"

"You're different."

"Thank you...I think." She squinted at me.

"He's always telling Mom it's time she moved on. I don't want her to move anywhere. And he never plays ball with me."

"Now, that's a serious charge!"

"And he lives in Ryewood!"

"It's getting worse by the minute."

"I mean it."

"I know you do." She sat beside Ali and began feeding her. After two spoonfuls, Ali clamped her mouth shut, insisting on feeding herself. A minute later her face and the high chair were covered with peas and mashed potatoes. "Sol should be here to see

17

this. He wouldn't feel so bad about living three thousand miles away from his own sloppy grandchildren."

"Dad and Marie never argue," I said, helping myself to chicken, "and they seem happy together."

"I hope they are. Both your parents deserve to be happy."

"Why'd Mom and Dad have to get divorced, anyway?" I asked.

"You're full of serious thoughts tonight, aren't you."

"None of my friends' parents are divorced. You and Sol are still married. It's not fair. Why do mine have to be the only ones?"

"They're not the only ones, I'm sorry to say. In my day it was pretty rare, but these days it's all the fashion. Just look at Hollywood. You're not a proper movie star without three or four weddings under your belt."

"Then what's the point of getting married if you're only going to mess it up?"

"Most folks don't plan on 'messing it

up,'" she said, scooping up some of the peas and trying to feed them to Ali. "Sometimes it just happens. People change as they get older. Sometimes their love deepens, sometimes it doesn't. It's not necessarily anyone's fault. That's just the way life is—always full of surprises."

"If Mom marries Arthur, they'll probably just end up getting divorced, too."

"Why do you say that? Second marriages are often very good ones."

"I don't know." I really didn't know. I just had this feeling that Mom was always going to be divorced and I was always going to be wishing she and Dad would get back together again.

Ali began banging her spoon on the high-chair tray and shouting, "Down! Ali down!"

"You're not finished yet, little Miss Impatience, not by a long shot. Look at all that perfectly good food."

Ali pushed her plate away. "No like chicken."

"You've got to have your protein," Helaine insisted, trying to spoon-feed her.

19

Ali pushed the spoon away, grabbed the pieces of chicken on her tray, and held her hand out over the edge.

"Alison Guttman," Helaine cried, "don't you dare!"

Ali looked at me, grinned, and opened her fingers, dropping the chicken at Helaine's feet.

"Brazen little beast," Helaine said, trying not to smile. "We do not throw our food on the floor." She leaned over with a groan and collected the chicken, then wiped Ali's face with a wet cloth. "You're a sight. Who'd ever guess that under all that food lies a face as pretty as your mama's."

"Want Mommy."

"Will you settle for this?" Helaine asked, handing her a lollipop.

Ali grabbed it. Helaine wiped her hands, lifted her from the high chair, and set her on the floor. Ali toddled out of the kitchen and sat on the steps in the front hall.

I tried to eat a few mouthfuls of chicken as I thought about Mom and Arthur and the opening game, but it just seemed to lie in my mouth, dry and tasteless. Finally I asked Helaine, "If I were your son, and the season opener was scheduled for the first night of Passover, would you let me play?"

Helaine picked up a drumstick. "If you were my son..." She paused and took a big bite of chicken, chewing thoughtfully.

"What?" I asked after a moment.

"I think I better mind my own business."

"Helaine! Come on. You'd let me play, wouldn't you?"

"The first night of Passover?"

"What's the big deal? It's just a big, boring dinner."

"Seder? Boring? What are you, some kind of Jewish Scrooge? It's the most delicious holiday we've got, and it's fun. How often do you get to go on a scavenger hunt during dinner?"

"Big deal!"

"And sing."

"I hate those songs."

"And enjoy good company."

"They're all Mom's friends, not mine."

"You *are* a Scrooge!"

21

"I want to play baseball," I complained. "Can't you talk to Mom for me? She'd listen to you."

Helaine clamped her hand over her mouth and pretended to padlock it.

"Jim Cohen's parents are letting *him* play. Come on, Helaine!"

"I'm afraid you'll have to fight this battle alone."

"Thanks a lot," I said, looking down at my plate. "I thought you were my friend."

"That's the oldest line in the book," she said, poking me in the ribs again.

Mom was asleep when I tiptoed into her room the next morning. Ali had climbed out of her crib during the night and lay beside her, wearing her footed duck pajamas, her face pressed up against her teddy bear. I stood at the end of the bed, expecting Mom to stir. She usually sensed me the moment I entered the room and woke up. But not this time. She must have gotten home late. I watched her and Ali sleeping, both breathing heavily. They looked alike. Mom's hair was longer and not as light as Ali's, but they had the same high forehead and the same almost-invisible eyebrows.

"I'm going to practice," I finally whispered. Mom rolled over, mumbled, "Be careful, sweetheart," and fell back asleep.

On my way to the field I stopped at Jim's house. He hopped down his back steps with an unpeeled banana between his teeth, a sneaker in one hand, his mitt in the other. His shirttails were out, and his other sneaker was unlaced. Lots of kids made fun of him because he was fat, but he was one of our best hitters and very fast for someone so big. He led the team in stolen bases. We'd been best friends since second grade.

"So what happened?" he asked, sitting on the curb to lace up his sneaker. His mitt fell open, revealing two chocolate bars. He handed me one. "Is your mom gonna let you play?"

"I'm pitching, no matter what she says," I insisted.

"She said no?"

"I'm not giving up."

"Did you tell her I'm playing?"

"Yeah. It didn't help. You're so lucky! I wish I had your parents."

"Sometimes I wish I had yours," he said.

"Yeah, sure! Like when?"

"Like when we have to go to temple Friday nights for the family service. You never have to go."

"We go sometimes. I'd rather do that than have to go to a seder any day."

He finished tying one sneaker and started on the other, eating at the same time. "Then you gotta try and make her feel real guilty or something," he muttered through a mouthful of banana.

"How?"

"Tell her the opener's the most important game of the season, maybe of your life. It could mean your whole career."

"I did."

"What'd she say?"

"No dice."

He thought a minute, finishing the banana. "Did you tell her it makes you feel happier than anything else in your whole life?"

25

"No. Well, sort of. I don't know." Mom knew I loved to play baseball. Why else would I spend so much time at it?

"Well, you gotta tell her. If she doesn't let you play, it's like she doesn't care if you're happy or sad."

"All she cares about is herself," I muttered, getting angry all over again.

"Tell her the only time you feel really happy is out on the mound."

"It's true," I said, suddenly feeling sorry for myself.

"And that you'll never complain again about having to get up early on Sundays for religious school if she lets you play, and you'll pay more attention to your Hebrew lessons."

"Yeah! That's a good idea."

Jim raised both hands and said, "High five."

I slapped his palms.

"We're gonna smear Ryewood this year," he said, tucking in half his shirt and jumping on his bicycle.

"I'm gonna shut 'em out."

26

"Hornets are number one!" he shouted, standing on his pedals and raising his fist in the air.

When we arrived at the field, Coach was liming the baselines while Mr. Duffy, our assistant coach, unloaded bats and balls from the trunk of his car. All that winter I'd spent three afternoons a week practicing my pitching with Coach Resnick. Sometimes I wished I had *him* for a father. He understood me a lot better than Mom or Dad did. When I told Dad I wanted to be a professional pitcher when I grew up, he smiled and said, "Only one in a million makes the majors, kiddo." Mom thought baseball was a nice way to "get a little fresh air and some exercise," nothing more. But Coach knew it was more important than that. He'd played in the minors after college and might have been signed by a major league team if he hadn't injured his elbow. He was the only adult I knew who took my love of baseball seriously. And he thought I showed real promise. At least, that's what he told me sometimes after a good practice: "There's real promise in that arm of yours, Danny."

I'd been the team's second-string pitcher most of last year, behind Timmy Sargent, but by the end of the season Coach had started me twice, saying I was developing a solid fastball and good control. I always played my best when he coached. Mom rarely came to my games, complaining they were either too early Saturday mornings or too late weekday afternoons. Dad appeared only once or twice a season, when he and Marie weren't traveling. The only one I could count on was Helaine. She and Sol came to lots of games and always sat in the first row of the bleachers, eating popcorn out of a big cardboard bucket. But what mattered most was that Coach was there. The one game he missed last year turned out to be my worst. I walked eight batters and beaned one. Mr. Duffy yanked me after three innings.

But Coach would be there for the opener, and so would I. After all the time he'd spent helping me, I couldn't tell him, "I'm sorry. My mom says I have to go to a seder instead."

"How's the arm?" Coach shouted from the right-field line.

I swung it over my head. "Feels good."

"No injuries before Thursday, please."

Jim and I tossed a ball back and forth as the rest of the team arrived, dumping their bicycles in the grass and hurrying onto the field. Coach led us through warm-ups, his black cleats kicking up puffs of dirt as he jogged around the bases. Then he sent us to our positions and hit fly balls and grounders to us.

"Man on first, no outs," he shouted, smacking the ball deep into right field. Jim raced forward and caught it but forgot about the man on first, throwing it to me on the mound.

"Wake up, Mr. Cohen!" Coach yelled. "I said, 'Man on first.' He just tagged up and made second."

Picking up another ball, he called, "Man on second, one out." This time he hit a hard bouncer to third. Matty checked the imaginary runner at second, then hurled the ball to first.

"Out!" Coach cried. "Nice work, Matt." Mr. Duffy applauded from the sidelines.

Each time Coach tossed the ball in the air, my heart pounded as I wondered if it would come to me. He popped the third hit to short center. Daryl dove, dropped the ball, then threw down his mitt in anger.

"No tantrums, Mr. Deagan. I want a disciplined ball club, not prima donnas."

His next hit was a sacrifice bunt that dribbled a few feet from the plate. I raced forward, scooped up the ball with my left hand, and fired it toward first. The throw went over Bobby's head.

"Safe at first," Coach called. "Don't be so anxious, Danny. Take time to aim." I nodded without looking him in the eye.

When we split into two teams for a practice game, I pitched for one side, Timmy for the other. Coach umped from behind the plate. Twice he stepped up to bat himself, forcing us to make difficult plays. When he

did, I pitched as hard as I could, trying to strike him out. But he could hit the ball no matter where I put it, even when it was wildly high and outside. At one point he smashed my fastest pitch high over Brian's head and yelled, "Wake up out there, Hogan! This is baseball, not butterfly collecting."

After five innings, he sat us down in the shade, picked up his clipboard, and began discussing the opening game while Mr. Duffy passed around oranges.

"Starting team for Thursday, you know who you are." We nodded. "I know some of you may have a conflict with Passover that day. I'm sorry about the scheduling. Let me know during Monday practice if you can't make it."

When the noon siren sounded, Coach reminded us that we had a short strategy session Wednesday afternoon to prepare for the Ryewood game, then sent us home. "Keep that arm warm," he told me as I climbed onto my bicycle. "And, Jim, lay off the chocolate bars awhile."

Mom and Ali were out back watering the vegetable patch when I returned home. Ali ran over to show me her sandals.

"New sues," she said, pointing proudly.

"Very pretty," I answered, dropping onto the grass.

"Flowers," she said, holding out a fistful of wilting dandelions. The lawn was covered with them.

"It almost feels like summer," Mom said, brushing the hair away from her forehead with the back of her hand. Her fingers and forearms were streaked with dirt. She'd spent the morning planting neat rows of peas and string beans, cucumbers and tomatoes. "How was the game?"

"It wasn't a game, just practice," I said, yanking a dandelion from the grass. I couldn't believe she'd already forgotten that the first game wasn't until Thursday.

"Hungry?" she asked.

"Yeah."

"Grilled cheese or hot dog?"

"Cheese," Ali said.

"I know what you want, you little mouse," she said, tickling Ali.

"I don't care," I muttered.

"Well, when you've decided, let me know." She leaned over and straightened the sticks marking the freshly planted rows. "Isn't nature amazing?" she reflected. "You plant something the size of a grain of sand, and a few months later you harvest bushels of beans. Imagine being the first person to discover you could do that." She blew a dandelion puff at me. "Isn't that *awesome*?"

I grunted, looking the other way.

"Just think about it. I mean, suppose I came up to you and said, 'Here, take this.'" She took my hand and placed a tiny black seed no bigger than the head of a pin in the center of my palm. "Stick this tiny nothing in the ground, pour a little water over it, and in a few weeks—poof!—you won't be hungry anymore. What do you think people said in the beginning? 'Get outta here! No way! You're bonkers!'" She tried to tickle me.

"Mom!" I griped.

"Loosen up, soldier."

"I don't like getting tickled."

"Am I tickling you?" she asked, raising her hands in the air.

I tried not to smile.

"Ellen invited us over after lunch."

"Do I have to go?"

"You got other plans?"

"There's nothing to do there."

"So bring something. Did you finish your homework?"

"No."

"Do it there. It's a beautiful day. We'll all sit out on the terrace and enjoy the sun. Maybe Arthur'll join us."

"Arthur! You just saw him last night."

"So? Did I use up my weekly ration?"

"How come you only go out with him now? What's so special about Arthur?"

"He's thoughtful and bright and funny. We share a lot of interests. I guess I just feel very comfortable with him."

"You argue with him sometimes."

"I argue with you, too. That doesn't mean I don't love you. Arthur's a little set in his ways, but so am I."

"Does that mean you're gonna marry him?"

"How would you feel if I did?" she asked, squinting at me. Ali sat down between us and began pulling her dandelions apart. A bumblebee buzzed overhead.

"I bet he wishes you didn't have kids."

"How can you say that? He's crazy about you two!"

"Oh, sure! He's always taking you out, never us. And all he ever says to me is 'How ya doin', Danny boy'! I hate it when he calls me that."

"Since when did you get so touchy?" Mom asked with her fake frown. "He's just trying to be friendly. He doesn't spend a lot of time around kids anymore, not since his grew up, but he loves you two." She laid her hand on my knee.

"Why can't you and Dad just get back together?" I asked.

Mom laughed bitterly. "In case you hadn't noticed, your father already has a wife." She shook her head and threw a dandelion stem into the bushes. "I know how you feel, Danny. Sometimes I can't believe this is my life. I never imagined I'd be the divorced mother of two children. I grew up thinking marriage lasted forever. No one got divorced when I was a kid. Maybe some parents weren't that happy together, but they stuck it out. Now everyone has second husbands, second wives, stepchildren, stepbrothers, half sisters, half a dozen grandparents, two homes—and they're still not happy. I hope your generation finds a better solution."

"I'm never getting married," I declared, leaning back on my elbows and feeling the warm sun on my face.

Mom smiled. "You may change your mind in a few years." Then she grew quiet and thoughtful, her forehead creasing the way it did when she had a headache.

"I heard some interesting news from Ellen this morning," she said reluctantly.

Ellen again! I watched Ali pulling up more dandelions.

"You're going to have another little brother or sister."

"What?" A wave of anger shot through me as though someone had hit me from behind.

"Don't look at me like that," Mom said, surprised. "It's not my fault."

"What are you talking about?" I asked.

"Ellen heard from a friend of hers who knows Marie that your father and step-mother are expecting a baby."

I groaned.

"What's the matter?" Mom asked.

"That's awful," I said.

"Don't tell your father that." She smiled.

"It's not funny, Mom."

"I know," she said, growing serious again. "I thought you'd take it hard."

"What does he need to have more children for?" I asked. "He's got us."

"I guess Marie wants a child of her own."

"It's not fair," I said, feeling tears come to my eyes.

"What's not?"

"My life!" I replied, almost shouting. "Everything's going wrong." I pulled up a fistful of grass and hurled it at the sky. Ali imitated me.

"Not the grass," Mom scolded her, "just the dandelions." But Ali kept at it, looking at Mom to see what she'd do. Mom glared at her a moment, then ignored her.

"I hardly ever get to see Dad," I complained. "Once he has a new baby, he'll just forget about us."

"He will not." Mom threw an arm

around my shoulder. "He's your father. He loves you. And he has responsibilities that I'd make sure he didn't neglect."

"How?" I challenged her. "What if he and Marie decide to take their baby and move away? You couldn't stop them."

"Your father has no intention of moving away. He purposely found a house in the area so he could be near you."

"That was before. Everything could change now."

"It won't, believe me. He wants all his children to grow up knowing one another."

"How do you know?"

"I just spoke to him."

"He said that?"

"Yup."

The knot in my stomach began to ease.

"You'll be a great big brother. You already are with Ali. And who knows, maybe this one will be a boy. Wouldn't that be fun, a little brother to teach baseball to?"

"When will it be born?" I asked.

"Not until September."

That seemed years away. Nothing had to

change for a while at least. I lay back in the grass, using my hands for a pillow.

"Feeling better?" Mom asked.

"I guess." One minute the worst thing in the world was the thought of Mom marrying Arthur, then it was having to miss the season opener, and now it was this new baby. "How'd you feel when Ellen told you?" I asked Mom.

"Strange at first. Then half-angry, half-jealous. And now happy."

"Why were *you* angry?"

"Because having babies with your father was the most wonderful thing I ever did, and this new baby of his won't be mine. But it will be *ours,* and that's lovely to think about."

"If you married Arthur, would you want to have more kids, too?" I asked, getting worried all over again.

"Oh, God. You're way ahead of me. First I have to decide if I want to get remarried."

"Do you?"

"I don't know," Mom replied, taking Ali on her lap. She grew thoughtful.

"You've got us," I reminded her.

She took my hand. "I know I do, but you'll both grow up one day, go off to college, settle down. You've got your own lives to live. I need someone who'll remain behind with me."

"Mom, I'm not even twelve yet."

"You were Ali's age a moment ago. Now look at you, practically shaving."

"Mom!"

She ruffled my hair. "You two are the best thing that ever happened to me."

"And you're the best mom."

"You really mean that?" she asked.

"Well, you're strict sometimes," I said, realizing this was probably the perfect time to bring up the game again and make her feel guilty, like Jim suggested. But I didn't have the heart to.

"It's not easy being a parent," she said sadly.

"You're doing okay, Mom."

She gave me a crooked smile. "*Okay?* A minute ago I was the best mom."

"You know what I mean."

"I think so," she said, kissing the end of my nose. "Hot dog or grilled cheese?"

"Grilled cheese."

"We're making progress," she said, rising.

"Did Arthur ask you to marry him?" I asked, sitting up.

"No."

"Would you, if he did?"

"I don't know. I'm not sure what I want."

"I know what I want," I said, following her toward the kitchen.

"Danny!" She turned and glared at me.

"I just want you to be happy, Mom," I said, pretending that was all I meant to say.

She smiled and threw her arms around me. "I thought you were about to mention baseball."

"Who? Me?"

E llen lived in a big house with a tennis court and a swimming pool. We found her lying on a beach chair on the stone terrace overlooking the pool. She was surrounded by manuscripts and books. Ellen was always reading. Mom said she was a very successful literary agent who represented lots of famous writers.

"Did you bring a suit?" Ellen asked, pointing toward the empty pool. Two men were painting the inside with wide rollers on long poles.

"I can't believe it's almost that time again," Mom said, dropping into a chair beside her.

"Could snow tomorrow, you never know. 'April is the cruelest month.'"

"Cheery thought."

"How you doing, Danny?" Ellen asked.

"Okay," I mumbled.

"You broke the news?" Ellen asked Mom.

"About Marie? Yes. He knows. That's not the problem. Danny's annoyed with me and the whole Jewish world for scheduling Passover on the night of his opening game."

"And Marty Resnick didn't kick up a fuss?" Ellen asked. "I'm surprised at him."

"You know Coach?" I asked.

"We went to high school together," she replied. "Can't he do anything?"

"Nope."

"I wish Danny didn't have to miss it," Mom said. "It's not fair to him and the other Jewish kids. But what can I do? Passover comes first."

"Who are you playing?" Ellen asked.

"Ryewood," I muttered.

"Ryewood? You'll kill 'em."

"I wish I could," I said, surprised by her enthusiasm.

"There'll be other games," Mom said, trying to make me feel better.

"There won't be another opener against Ryewood," I said. I looked at Ellen, hoping she might help me convince Mom. But just at that moment Ali reached the top step of the terrace.

Ellen reached for her. "Come here, you golden dumpling, and give your aunt Ellen a kiss."

Ali squirmed, demanding to be put down, then headed for the opposite end of the terrace and the empty pool.

"No, Ali!" Mom cried, running after her. "That's dangerous. You could fall in. You stay right here on the terrace with us." She moved an empty chair in front of the steps. The painters looked up at us from the bright white bottom of the pool. One of them waved. Ali waved back.

"Swim?" Ali asked.

"Not today," Mom said. "Maybe next time."

Ellen's cat, Boots, wandered onto the terrace. He rubbed himself against a chair leg but darted away when Ali tried to pet him. Ali chased after him, calling, "Boots, Boots."

"Where are the girls?" Mom asked. Ellen had two daughters, thirteen and fifteen.

"With Peter. It's his weekend." Peter was Ellen's ex-husband.

"No wonder it's so quiet."

"Divorce has its benefits," Ellen replied with a bitter laugh.

"Richard wants the kids more often," Mom said, referring to Dad, "but I don't want to give them up, especially on the weekends."

"Peter's always changing his plans and disappointing either the girls or me." She frowned a moment, then pushed herself up from her chair. "There aren't any easy solutions, are there? Well, who wants something to drink? I've got soda in the kitchen and chips in the pantry and grapes, lots of grapes!"

"No thanks," I said sullenly, hoping to get the conversation back to my game.

"Danny, don't sulk," Mom scolded. "We're guests here."

"I just don't want anything," I complained.

"That's okay," Ellen replied, turning toward the kitchen.

"If you don't feel like being social," Mom said, "then go off somewhere and do your homework."

"Fine," I said, grabbing my backpack and heading to the back of the garden.

"Danny," Mom called, sounding suddenly sorry. But I pretended not to hear her. I walked past the pool to what had once been an apple orchard. Most of the trees looked as if they were dying. Their black branches were gnarled and withered. A few, though, had sprouted white blossoms that fluttered to the ground whenever the wind blew. I dropped my pack in the tall grass and leaned back against a fallen tree, out of sight of the terrace. The new grass smelled of onions. Dandelions grew everywhere.

"Next time I'm staying home," I muttered, pulling out my math book. I threw it on the grass, dug out a pencil, then lay on my stomach and began reading the word problems. Almost instantly I forgot my anger. I liked math. Each time I solved a difficult problem, it made me feel good, like catching the inside corner of the plate with my fastball.

I finished the four I was assigned and was about to do one for extra credit when something moved through the grass. A small brown rabbit stood a few feet away, chewing on clover. He stopped eating when I lifted my head, his ears up, sensing danger. I lay still. His nose twitched, sniffing the air. After a moment he went back to his chewing, then dropped his head back into the lawn. I set my book down and crept toward him. Wouldn't it be great to lose yourself in the grass, I thought. The rabbit sensed me and hopped a few feet away, paused a moment, and darted into a thick hedge and disappeared.

The sprouting grass was thick with last fall's rotting apples. I picked one up and hurled it against a distant tree trunk, hitting it square in the center.

"Strike!" I declared.

How could I convince Mom to let me play? I wondered. There had to be something I could say to change her mind. Half the school would be at the opener, cheering us on. It was my chance to shine, to show everyone how good I'd become in the last year. I picked up another apple and shattered it against the same tree trunk.

"Nice pitch," a voice said. Arthur approached from the pool. He wasn't wearing his usual sport jacket but neatly pressed jeans, a polo shirt, sneakers, and a baseball cap! From a distance, with his white hair covered, he looked almost as young as Coach.

"Some place, isn't it?" Arthur said.

"Yeah," I said flatly.

"Must have been really beautiful once." He crouched down beside a dead-looking branch that had blossomed in the grass and lifted it to his nose. I took a good look at him. He wasn't really so old. I just never liked the idea that Mom was going out with anyone other than Dad, even after Dad married Marie. It didn't seem right.

"Your mom feels terrible about your missing the first game," he said, glancing toward me.

"Then she ought to let me play," I complained.

"Passover means a lot to her."

"And this game means a lot to me. She doesn't have to come to the game if she doesn't want to."

"I don't think that's the point," he said, picking up an apple and hurling it toward the same tree. It struck just below mine and splattered.

"Nice shot," I said, grudgingly.

He smiled. "I played baseball when I was your age. Ever hear of the Brooklyn Dodgers?"

"Yeah," I said flatly.

"They played in my backyard, Ebbets Field. I used to go to all their home games with my dad. He was a big fan."

"I bet they played on Passover."

"They probably did, but there weren't a lot of Jewish players in the league." He took out a handkerchief and wiped his hands. "It's not just that your mom wants to go to the seder, it's important that you be there with her. That's what Passover is all about, passing tradition from one generation to the next."

"I know all about Passover," I said, resenting his explanation. "I've been to seders ever since I was born."

"Me too," he said. "But I learn something new each time."

"Yeah, like what?" I challenged.

"Well..." He thought a moment. "Last year, for instance, I finally understood why the youngest child is supposed to ask the Four Questions instead of one of the older kids."

I didn't really care why.

"It's to welcome youngsters into the seder," he said after a moment, "to make them feel a part of it and of Jewish history. Even more than that, it reminds the old folks like me that one day that little voice will be leading the seder. Our lives are short, but the life of the Jewish people is never ending. That's kind of neat, don't you think?"

"I don't know." I wasn't really listening. I was thinking about his marrying Mom and what it would be like having a stepfather whose kids were already in college.

"Did you like going to seders when you were my age?" I asked.

He smiled. "Honestly? Not really. I had an uncle who was something of a biblical scholar. He used to conduct the entire seder in Hebrew. It wasn't until I got to college and started attending other seders that I understood what it was all about and began to enjoy it."

"Did your kids like it?"

"I think the older they got, the more

they appreciated it, but you'd have to ask them. Maybe they're just humoring their old man."

What I really wanted to know was whether or not he was going to propose to Mom, but I didn't feel comfortable asking him straight out, and I suppose a part of me really didn't want to know. So I turned back to my math book.

"Homework?" he asked.

"Yeah."

"What's your favorite subject?"

"Math, I guess."

"Really? History was mine, especially the Civil War. My father once took me to visit some of the old battlefields. I was hooked after that. You could almost see the men coming up over the hills, their rifles and sabers flashing in the sunlight. You ever been to one?"

"Nope."

"You think that would interest you?"

Was he asking if I wanted to go with him sometime, as if I were his son? "I already have a father," I blurted out angrily.

He looked surprised for a moment but replied very calmly, "Yes, you do."

"And I'd never want to move to Ryewood or anyplace else," I added, my pent-up feelings suddenly spilling out. "All my friends live here. I hate Ryewood."

"I don't think anyone's asking you to," he replied gently. "But for what it's worth, I think I know how you feel. When I was your age, my father got transferred. We had to move across the country. It was the worst year of my life."

"I wouldn't have gone," I insisted.

He smiled. "I didn't have much choice. Change is tough sometimes, but it's pretty hard to avoid. Look at you, getting more independent, improving your pitching, growing up. Pretty soon you'll be wanting to make lots of changes yourself."

He seemed to know exactly what was on my mind but wasn't answering my question.

"Danny," Mom called from the terrace.

"What?" I yelled back.

"Thirsty?"

"Nope."

"Arthur?"

"Not just yet," he replied.

Arthur sat on the fallen apple tree beside me, took out a small pocketknife, and cut off two small branches covered with white apple blossoms. "You've got a lot to contend with just now, I know," he said. "I'll try not to further complicate your life."

I turned and looked at him, embarrassed by my outburst. He smiled and winked at me, then got up as Mom and Ali appeared.

"What are you two desperadoes plotting back here?" she asked.

Arthur handed them the apple branches.

"Bunny!" Ali said, pointing to the bushes. The rabbit had returned to the edge of the grass. "Need bunny!" Ali said, trying to pull free of Mom's arm.

"Shh! Don't scare it away," Mom whispered, putting a finger to her lips.

"Bunny!" Ali insisted. She struggled, but Mom held tight.

"Look at the pretty flowers, Ali," I said,

trying to divert her attention with the apple blossoms. But she wouldn't be distracted. Arthur knelt down and with the quickness of a magician pretended to pull a penny from her ear.

"Look what Ali has growing in her ear," he said, showing it to her. But she saw only the bunny.

Finally Mom set her free. Ali hurried toward the rabbit. It glanced up at her and darted into the hedge.

"Need bunny," Ali repeated sadly.

"Sorry, sweetheart," Mom said. "Maybe it'll come back later."

"Need bunny now!"

I knew how Ali felt, wanting something just out of reach. I tried to think of some comforting words to say to her, but none came to mind.

"What inning is it?" Mom asked, dropping on the couch behind me. She had just put Ali to bed and changed into her nightgown and bathrobe. I lay on the floor watching the ball game, still thinking of new arguments to convince her to let me play.

"Top of the fifth," I answered.

She groaned, picked up a magazine, and began flipping through it. "Don't you ever get tired of watching that stuff?" she asked.

I shook my head. So far the game was a no-hitter. After another minute Mom asked, "What is it about baseball that people find so fascinating? Nothing's happening. One man throws the ball, then waits five minutes while everyone talks about it. Then he throws it again. It would drive me nuts."

"Every pitch is important," I explained.

"I thought the players were supposed to hit the ball and run around the bases, get a little exercise."

"He's pitching a great game."

"This is great?"

"Never mind, Mom."

"Want anything from the kitchen?" she asked, getting up. I shook my head. She left the room, made a few phone calls, and returned with a plate of orange slices. At the next commercial I turned around and faced her. I had my new argument all thought out. She offered me some orange. I shook my head.

"Mom?"

"Uh-oh! I know that 'Mom.'"

"If I was sick, would you make me get out of bed to go to the seder?"

"Of course not, Danny. That's silly. When a person's sick, all their usual obligations are suspended. But you're not sick."

"But what if I was?"

"Danny, please! You're not sick, and Passover is very important. It's our history, our religion, our community, the future—it's everything that's important to us as Jews. Even Arthur agrees with me on this one, and he appreciates baseball."

"Yeah, right! The Brooklyn Dodgers! I don't care what Arthur thinks. He's not my father."

"No, he's not, but he's a very sensible man." She sat back on the couch and helped herself to some orange. "Did you tell Coach you can't be at the game?"

"Nope."

"Doesn't he need to know?"

"I want to play!"

"Danny!"

"You don't care about anyone but yourself," I cried.

"That is *so* unfair. Everything I do is for you two. I wish I had a nickel for every time I've denied myself something to make you happy."

A part of me hated hurting her feelings—I knew how hard she worked, how much she did for us—but another part said she deserved it.

"We used to be a family when Dad lived here. Now you never have time for us. You're always going out."

"That is *not* true. Didn't we just have dinner together? Didn't I spend all afternoon with you? Aren't I sitting here now? Most parents I know, married or divorced, spend a lot less time with their children than I do. Maybe once a week I get a few hours to myself. Some weeks I don't even get that. I'm very sorry if that bothers you, but I need a life, too."

I knew she was right, but I couldn't give up, not as long as there was still a chance she'd let me play.

"Baseball is *my* life. There's nothing

more important to me. It's the only thing I have left."

Mom smiled.

"It's not funny, Mom," I complained. I hated when she didn't take me seriously. "I feel like an orphan sometimes. You never come to my games. Dad's always traveling."

"An orphan? Oh, please! You hardly qualify. I'm sorry about missing your games, but it's not easy running a household and having a career and taking care of two children. There just aren't enough hours in the day. When I get home, I just want to collapse. And Saturday mornings are the only time I can catch up on my sleep."

Her face twisted into one of her sarcastic smiles. "Orphan! For your information, I'm just as concerned as you are about our family. That's one of the reasons why celebrating the seder together is so important. We need to do more things as a family. That's what being Jewish is all about—family."

"Without Dad, it doesn't feel like a family, no matter how many seders we have."

"Danny, lots of parents get divorced. It's not the end of the world. Frankly, I think we're doing pretty well, considering."

"I don't," I sulked.

"Come here," she said, extending her arms toward me.

"Why?" I said, resisting.

"Just get over here and give your old mom a hug."

Reluctantly I pushed myself up from the floor and sat down next to her with my arms crossed.

"Oh, come on, don't be such a sourpuss." She jabbed me in the ribs, trying to make me smile. I moved away, keeping my eyes on the television.

"I was a kid once, too, you know. I understand how you feel."

"Yeah, sure," I replied. "You never played baseball."

"No, but I once was just as much in love with ice-skating as you are with baseball."

"So?"

"So, you think you're the only one who

dreams of greatness? When I was your age, I wanted to be the next Peggy Fleming. Know who she is?"

I shook my head.

"Only one of the world's most famous figure skaters."

"Big deal."

"Big deal! She won the Olympic gold medal. She was beautiful and talented, and every girl skater dreamed of being just like her. From November to April I spent practically every Saturday on the ice. And every year I performed in the big ice show at the end of the season. It was the most important event of the year for me."

"Only one year you had to go to a dumb seder instead, right?"

"Wrong! But you're close. My cousin Larry's bar mitzvah. I cried for days, threw tantrums, even threatened to run away— you haven't tried that one yet—then I sulked for weeks. I'd practiced all winter. And it wasn't like there was another show the next day or the next week, or a whole season to look forward to. There was only one performance a year, and I had to miss it."

"You should have run away," I grumbled.

"I planned to. I was gonna join the Ice Capades." She shook her head, smiling. "I even packed a bag and told my best friend I was leaving."

Against my will I listened, but I kept my eyes on the ball game. It was still a no-hitter.

"As I lay in my warm bed every night, feeling sorry for myself, it was exciting to think about running away, but the next morning the idea always seemed a little frightening."

"So what happened?"

"Nothing. I kept badgering my parents, hoping they'd change their minds right up to the moment we got in the car to drive to Long Island. I cried all the way to the synagogue, but then my cousin Sally arrived, and we spent the whole service whispering to each other about how mean our parents were—hers wouldn't let her take horseback-riding lessons; they thought it was too dangerous. I felt a lot better after that and actually enjoyed the party."

"I'm gonna hate the seder," I said.

"You may be surprised," she said with a mischievous look.

"The only thing that would surprise me is if you let me play."

My eyes were fixed on the TV. The pitcher wound up and released the ball. Even with the sound way down I heard the crack of the bat, a single to short left field. There went the no-hitter. I groaned.

"What's the matter?" Mom asked.

"Nothing," I muttered. "You wouldn't understand."

"Oh, come on, Danny, don't be like that. Just because you love someone doesn't mean you always agree. If I didn't care about you, I'd probably say, sure, go play your game, do whatever you like, it's all the same to me. But I *do* love you—"

"Then—"

"Let me finish. And because I care, I want you to do what's right, which isn't always what you want. It wasn't what I wanted either, and it took me a long time before I realized that my parents were right. Preserving our Jewish heritage—going to bar mitzvahs and seders—is more important than ice-skating or baseball."

I sat staring at the screen sullenly, trying to think up another argument, but Mom wasn't finished. She'd been thinking about all this just as much as I had.

"You know who Sandy Koufax is, right?" she asked.

"No, Mom, never heard of him," I said sarcastically.

"Arthur told me he won all these awards."

"Three-time Cy Young Award winner, held the record for most strikeouts in a season until Nolan Ryan beat him by one; threw the greatest curveball in history."

"He was Jewish, you know."

"Everybody knows that."

"And do you know that one year the World Series fell on Yom Kippur?"

"Yeah, and he didn't pitch," I said, knowing exactly what she was going to say.

"Do you know why?"

"Because it was a Jewish holiday," I replied, mimicking her voice.

"Not just any Jewish holiday," she corrected, "but the holiest day of the Jewish year."

I looked toward the television just as another batter connected, driving the ball over the right-field wall. The pitcher was coming apart. I slammed my fist into the arm of the couch.

"Danny!"

"What a choke," I complained, angry at Mom, angry at the pitcher, angry at Sandy Koufax for not playing in the World Series. "Coach worked all winter with me."

"I'm sorry, sweetheart."

"You're not sorry!" I cried, standing up. "Just because your parents wouldn't let you skate, you won't let me play. It's not fair."

"It's not a question of what's fair but of what's right. I just explained that."

"If I lived with Dad, *he'd* let me play."

"That's entirely possible," Mom said, shaking her head. "But you don't live with your father."

"Well, maybe I should," I said with my hands on my hips.

"It sure beats running off to join the Ice Capades," she said.

"Don't treat me like a baby!" I snapped, then turned and left the room. "I'm playing in that game," I yelled from the front hall, "even if I have to run away from home to do it!"

I ran up the stairs and dropped on my bed. I'd call Dad first thing in the morning. He'd understand. He and Marie would be glad to have me. He didn't care about going to seders; he just wanted me to be happy. That's what he always said: "Danny, life's tough enough without families fighting. I just want you to be happy."

After a few minutes, Mom knocked and opened my door. "I guess I shouldn't expect you to understand all this, but you will someday."

"I'm playing in that game," I declared one last time.

She ignored my remark and asked, "Would you like to call Coach Resnick, or should I?"

"I'm not calling him."

"Very well, I will," she said, closing the door behind her.

"Mom!" Tears of rage sprang to my eyes. "I hate you!" I grabbed my overnight bag from the closet and began throwing clothes into it. Five minutes later, Mom stuck her head back in.

"Where do you think you're going?" she asked.

"To Dad's."

"Your father's leaving for Europe tomorrow."

"Then I'll go with him to Europe."

"Danny, don't be silly."

"I'm not staying here," I insisted.

Mom put on her tight, tense face. "Coach Resnick said he was sorry you wouldn't be playing and hopes the same problem won't arise next year. He was very understanding. And he wishes you a happy Passover." She shut the door.

I reached into my bag, grabbed a sweater, and threw it across the room, followed by my pants, socks, and sneakers. Then I picked up my mitt and hurled it into the closet.

I skipped practice Monday and avoided the gym. I couldn't face Coach after all he'd done for me. I didn't think I'd ever be able to look him in the face again. One minute Mom was telling me I was old enough to take on adult responsibilities like watching Ali while she ran to the post office, the next minute she was treating me like a baby, forcing me to do what *she* wanted. I didn't even feel like watching baseball on TV. Just thinking about it made me angry. How come everyone else could play in Thursday's game? It wasn't fair. I wanted to run away.

When I got home Monday afternoon, Mom and Ali were just pulling into the driveway.

"You're back early," Mom said. "Aren't you supposed to be at practice?"

"What's the point if I can't play? I'm quitting the team."

I felt a sudden rush of power. I hadn't thought about quitting until that moment, but it suddenly seemed right.

"You're quitting the team?" Mom asked in her matter-of-fact voice. "*You*, Mr. Baseball, Mr. There-Is-Nothing-More-Important-in-This-Whole-World-than-Pitching Guttman? This I gotta see."

"I'm not kidding, Mom," I said, annoyed that she didn't take me seriously.

Instead of replying, she pulled Ali out of her car seat and set her on the driveway. Ali toddled toward the front steps, saying, "Dowa, dowa."

"It's just a waste of time, anyway," I added.

"Danny! Stop feeling sorry for yourself. You're missing one lousy game. You've got the whole season ahead of you. You've worked hard."

"I'm not playing."

Mom looked at me a moment. Ali called from the doorstep, "Dowa open!"

"What did Coach Resnick say when you told him you were quitting?" Mom asked, heading toward the house.

"I haven't told him yet."

"Don't you think you owe him an explanation? He's spent a lot of time with you."

"I only just decided."

"Oh, I see." She squinted at me with a crooked smile as she opened the door. The day's mail lay scattered on the floor below the mail slot. I tossed my backpack in the corner and followed Ali into the kitchen while Mom went through the mail.

"Letter from your father," she said, laying it aside on the counter. I always rushed to open Dad's letters, but this time I pretended not to care, letting it lie there while I poured myself some juice. I rinsed out my glass, grabbed an apple and the letter, and walked out to the swings, feeling Mom's eyes on me. I knew she was curious about what Dad had written. The letter said:

Dear Danny,

I'm sorry I didn't get a chance to see you before we left for England. But I spoke with Mom on the phone, and she told me about your baseball problem. I feel bad for you, slugger. I know how much the opener means to you. It was lousy of them to schedule it Thursday night. But Mom's right, seders are important. You probably don't think so now. I know I didn't when I was your age. But then, I didn't think much of school either, or piano lessons, or visiting my grandparents—and nothing my parents said ever convinced me otherwise. But I'm glad for all those things now. Marie and I will be attending a seder in Milan with old friends of mine from college. How's your Hebrew these

days? Mine's pretty rusty. I'll be thinking of you as we hide the afikoman. (Remember when it fell from the flowers into the vase and got all soggy?)

Whenever I'm faced with a disappointment like yours, I try to focus on the next big event, the next game, the rest of the season. Don't get stuck on the opener. If you guys do well, you might come up against Ryewood again in the play-offs. Then you'll shut them out. I'm looking forward to watching you pitch when we get back.

How about we take in a Yankees game this season? I'll call you as soon as we get home. Give your little sister a big hug from me. And wish Mom a happy Passover. Marie sends her love.

Love,
Dad

The last time Dad and I had gone to a ball game was just before he and Mom split up. It was one of the happiest moments of my life. I've often wondered if Dad already knew he and Mom were getting divorced as we sat there eating peanuts and hot dogs. I guess it doesn't matter. We had a great time, the Yankees won, and that's when I decided to become a major league pitcher. But now all that was over, Dad was remarried, and I was through with baseball.

"Danny, would you keep an eye on Ali while I run to the market?" Mom yelled from the window. "We're out of milk."

"Yeah," I called back. The screen door opened. Ali toddled out and climbed the three stone steps to the back of the garden, using her hands for balance. "Swing," Ali said, raising her arms.

I picked her up—she was getting heavy—and strapped her into her yellow plastic seat, then gave her a push. Her curly blond hair streamed backward and then forward, tickling her cheeks and making her laugh. I laughed, too. She looked so funny when the hair covered her face.

"Anything else we need?" Mom asked, standing by the back door.

I shrugged.

"How about pizza tonight?" she asked. "Might as well get in a major bread fix before Thursday."

"I don't care," I replied, trying not to look at her.

"Extra cheese?"

"Whatever you want."

"Cannoli?" A sly smile spread across her face.

"Coni," Ali said. She loved them.

"I know what you like, you little cream puff," Mom said. She looked at me.

"Yeah, okay," I said flatly.

"Any special news from your father?" she asked, glancing at the open letter in the grass.

"He and Marie are going to a seder in Italy," I said.

"Really?" she replied, walking to the swings. "Did he say anything about your game?"

"You can read it," I said.

"Only if you don't mind."

"I don't care."

She picked up Dad's letter and read quickly, nodding her head occasionally. "That's good advice," she finally said.

"What is?"

"About concentrating on the rest of the season instead of just the first game."

"I'm concentrating on going away to summer camp instead."

"It's only April."

"There's nothing else to look forward to until then."

"You could look forward to Thursday night. I know you don't think so, but you're gonna have a good time at the seder."

"Oh, sure."

"You'll see," she said with a wink, then left for the market.

"Mommy!" Ali called after her.

"She'll be right back," I said.

"Go Mommy," Ali shouted, stretching out her arms. "Down! Awi down." She kicked her legs in frustration.

I gave her swing a big push.

"No swing!" Ali insisted. "Down." And then she began to cry.

"Okay, don't get so excited," I said, releasing her. As soon as her feet touched the grass, she ran toward the driveway.

I jogged after her. "Mom's coming right back. She just went to the supermarket." Ali stood in the driveway crying. I picked her up, but she kicked and squirmed. When she was angry, the only way to quiet her was to get her to think about something else. "Want a cookie?" I asked. She shook her blond curls. "Juice?" I tried.

"No want juice!" she declared angrily.

"How about a walk?"

"Park," she said, taking my hand and heading for the street.

We walked alongside the curb, Ali stopping every few feet to pick up stones. I pointed to the yellow hedge in front of one house. "Look, Ali, spring." A patch of purple flowers had pushed through the grass. Ali wanted to pick them, as she had the dandelions, but I held her back and walked on. She strained against me, crying, "Need flowers." I dragged her along until a familiar car appeared in the distance, moving slowly toward us.

"Ali, look who's coming." I pointed to the bottom of the street. "Who's that?" Sol's old Studebaker approached, the sun reflecting off the chrome bumpers.

"Lane!" Ali cried.

Helaine stuck her hand out the passenger window and waved. "My two favorite kids in all the world!" she said as Sol stopped the car beside us. The old engine churned loudly.

"Is Mom going out tonight?" I asked, surprised to see her.

"Nope. We were just driving by." She opened her purse. "Look what I got here," she said, holding out two butterscotch candies. Ali reached up. I unwrapped them and gave her one.

"Where are you kids headed?" Sol asked. "Can I give you a lift?"

"We were just taking a walk," I said. "Ali

got upset when Mom left for the market, so I thought I'd take her to the park."

"Aren't you a loving big brother," Helaine said. "How about we walk with them?" she asked Sol. "We could use a little exercise."

"Fine by me," he replied, then pulled the car to the curb and shut off the engine. Ali took their hands, and they lifted her into the air between them.

"So, what's new?" Helaine asked me.

"Nothing."

"Nothing? Sounds serious. Still angry about the seder?"

I shrugged. I didn't want to talk about it. Helaine winked at Sol and turned her attention to Ali. When we reached the park, Ali broke away and ran to the slide. Helaine helped her up the ladder; Sol caught her at the bottom. I sat in the grass, watching a father pitch tennis balls to a boy about six years old. Each time the boy missed, his father said, "That's better. Keep your eye on the ball. You'll hit it." The dirt in front of the backstop was strewn with tennis balls. Every few minutes they gathered them up in a blue bucket and started over. The father was very patient, something Dad never was when he lived with us. He rarely played ball with me. He was always complaining he had too much work to do or his back was bothering him or he was just too tired. When he did play, he usually tried to get me to do things differently, to choke up on the bat or pitch with more shoulder, less wrist.

I inched over toward the father and son, wanting to join them. I would have been happy just to catch while the father pitched. I looked at my watch. Coach was probably breaking the team into two squads for a scrimmage just then. I wondered who was pitching against Timmy.

Just then the little boy connected with one of the tennis balls, sending it rolling toward me. "Thatta boy!" his father cried, full of pride. "You got it." I picked up the ball and threw it hard to the father, hoping he would invite me over. "Thanks," he called as the ball bounced out of his hand.

"Need a catcher?" I asked.

"We're just finishing up," he said, turning back to his son. He pitched the remaining balls. Then they gathered them up and left the park. I thought of Dad and his new baby. Would that be them in a few years? A sudden sadness washed over me, a combination of knowing Dad was so far away and that I was never going to play baseball again. I'd have to find something else to do with my life, but what? I didn't want to be a marketing consultant—whatever that was—like Mom, or a lawyer like Dad. I couldn't spend my life sitting in an office all day like I was in school. I wanted to be out on a ball field. I wanted people to know how good I was.

"Penny for your thoughts," Helaine said, easing herself down in the grass. Sol was pushing Ali on the swings.

"What did Sol use to do?" I asked.

"Do? My Solly? You mean work? As little as possible." She laughed.

"I mean it."

"He sold insurance, not very glamorous, but it paid the bills."

"Did he ever want to do anything else?"

"Like what—jump out of airplanes, climb Mount Everest? My Solly is nothing if not content. That could have been his middle name." She looked back toward Ali and Sol. "He was never a go-getter. He was happy to be the father of two girls, to be able to pay off the mortgage after thirty years, and to keep that chromium monstrosity of his running. He's a simple man."

"What do you think I ought to be when I grow up?"

"I thought that was already settled—another Sandy Koufax."

"I'm not playing anymore."

"What! Give up baseball? Come on."

"I mean it."

"Because of the seder?"

"It's not just that."

"What else?"

"I'll never be good enough."

"How do you know? You think Mr.

Koufax was born a champ? He had to work at it. You ask that handsome coach of yours. He'll tell you."

"Dad says only one in a million makes it."

"So, who says you can't be that one?"

"I just know," I said.

"You ever heard the expression 'Cutting off your nose to spite your face'?"

"What does that mean?" I asked.

"It means, don't do something that hurts *you* just to get back at someone else. You're angry at your mom for not letting you play, so you think you're gonna punish her by giving up baseball. Only you'll be the one who really suffers, because you love baseball. Think about it. You've got your whole career ahead of you."

"The whole thing's stupid."

"Baseball? Stupid?"

"It's just a game."

"So's the stock market, but that doesn't keep people from giving their whole lives and all their money to it. Maybe you should think about it awhile. Sleep on it."

"I've made up my mind. Anyway, no one really cares if I play."

"No one? What are we, chopped liver?" Helaine asked. "Did we miss a Saturday game last year?"

"I guess not."

"The correct answer is, no, Sol and Helaine, your most loyal fans, did not miss a single Saturday game. So, what's gonna be with us if you quit the team? Did you give that any thought?"

"You don't really care about my games," I insisted.

"Don't care?" she said with surprise. "Don't care? Sol, what are we gonna do with this boy?"

"What's the matter?" he asked, walking Ali slowly over to us.

"He's quitting the team."

"Really?"

"I'm not making it up."

"So, we get Ali to take his place," Sol declared, sitting down beside me. He pulled a dandelion from the grass, handed it to Ali, and told her to throw it. Ali's fat little wrist swung down. The flower fell in her lap.

"She'll need a little coaching," Sol said, laughing, "but I like her style."

"It's not funny." I got up. I was suddenly very angry.

"Danny, we were only kidding," Helaine explained.

"No, you weren't. Everyone thinks it's just a big joke."

"I wasn't laughing at you," Sol insisted.

"I don't care," I cried, and stormed out of the park.

A note was waiting for me in my classroom the next morning. I recognized
Coach's handwriting, and my heart began
to race. I didn't want to open it. He was
probably angry at me for missing practice.
We were supposed to let him know in ad-
vance when we couldn't be there. I stuffed
the note in my pocket just as Jim Cohen
came into the room.

"What happened to you yesterday?" he

asked, dropping his books and lunch on top of his desk.

"I'm quitting the team."

"You're *what*?"

"I'm not gonna play."

"Are you crazy? Why?"

"I'm just not, okay!"

"Are you in trouble or something? Did your mom ground you?"

"I don't wanna talk about it," I said, walking toward the door. I could feel Jim's eyes on me. I headed toward the cafeteria, trying to get lost in the crowd of kids just coming in from the bus. Coach Resnick was standing at the end of the hall, talking to one of the teachers. I felt the note in my pocket. The door to the AV room was open. I stepped inside and unfolded the paper. It said: "Please see me before lunch. Coach."

What was I going to say to him? "I'm quitting because I have to miss the opener"? It made me seem like such a jerk. He wasn't going to let me just walk off the team, not after all the time he'd spent

93

training me. If only I had some terrible disease or had broken my arm or had to move to another town.

The second bell rang. I had three hours to come up with a good excuse for quitting the team. I hurried back to my classroom and took my seat. My fifth-grade teacher, Mrs. Baron, began writing a long history assignment on the blackboard. I could feel Jim's eyes on me. I tried to ignore him. Out of the corner of my eye I saw him write something, fold it several times, and drop it near my feet. I let it lie there. He coughed. I kept my eyes on Mrs. Baron. He whispered, "Danny!" I ignored him.

"Jim, is something wrong?" Mrs. Baron asked.

"No."

"Save your note passing for lunch," she said, eyeing the slip of paper on the floor.

Jim reddened, leaned over, and picked it up. When Mrs. Baron turned back to the board, he tossed it onto my desk, then looked straight ahead. I slipped it into my pocket without opening it. Jim began fidgeting, tapping his pencil, his foot. When I looked at him, he was scowling at me, his chin pointing toward the hidden note. "Not now," I mouthed silently. But he insisted, jabbing the air with his index finger. I shook my head and looked away. A minute later another note appeared, this one open. I crumpled it up without looking at it and stuffed it in my desk.

"Jim and Danny, do I have to separate you?" Mrs. Baron asked.

"Sorry," Jim said sullenly. He left me alone after that. I avoided him when we went to music class and sat on the other side of the room during assembly. When the lunch bell rang, I ran out to the hall before Jim could catch me. He called, "Danny, wait up!" but I lost him in the lunch crowd. I had to think of something to tell Coach. His office was at the far end of school, next to the gym. I knew he was going to be angry with me. When he lost his temper on the ball field—which didn't happen often—there were fireworks. His face got red, and everyone became real quiet.

I knocked softly on his office door, my heart pounding. After a minute I knocked again, harder this time. Coach called, "Come in." He was sitting at his big wooden desk, writing up a practice schedule. The floor was crowded with bases and helmets and the catcher's gear. On a shelf behind him stood a dozen gold trophies with figures playing soccer, basketball, and baseball.

"Sit down, Danny," he said, pointing to a chair covered with playground balls. "Just throw those in the corner." When I sat down, he said, "What happened to you yesterday?"

I felt my arms and legs grow weak.

"I...uh...I'm not playing—"

"I know. Your mom called. I'm sorry about that."

Before I could tell him that I meant more than just Thursday, he pulled a sheet of paper from his desk drawer, studied it a moment, then looked across at me. "What do you think of Daryl as co-captain?"

"Daryl?" I was more surprised by the question than the choice. He was a good player, probably our best outfielder, and definitely our strongest hitter. But he had a bad temper. "I don't know. I guess he'd be okay."

"Could you work with him?" His mouth curved up into a faint smile.

"Me?" Was Coach saying he'd picked me to be the other captain? "Yeah. I guess, I mean..."

"You think he has the respect of the rest of the team?"

"He loses his temper a lot," I replied, my mind racing, "but he's our best all-around player."

Oh, God, I thought, how can I quit now? Co-captain! I'd never even dreamed of that! But I'd already told Mom I was leaving the team, and Jim and Helaine and Sol. If I didn't quit, Mom would never take me seriously again. I had to prove to her I meant what I said, that she couldn't treat me like a baby anymore. It was all her fault. If she wasn't going to let me play, then I wouldn't play at all, not even as co-captain.

"Coach?"

"Yes?"

"It's just that...well..." I looked down at my hands. "About yesterday. I just thought it didn't make any sense my coming...."

"Any sense?" His eyebrows came together in a puzzled look.

You can't stop now, I thought.

"I mean, what's the point of practicing if I'm quitting the team?"

"Quitting the team?" Coach repeated my words flatly, as if making sure he'd heard me correctly.

"I'll never be good enough to make the majors anyway. It's just a waste of time. My mom doesn't take it seriously. My dad's never around to watch me play." I suddenly felt like crying. I looked away and blinked my eyes until the stinging passed.

Coach watched me without speaking. When I looked back at him, he asked, "Have you discussed this with your mom?"

"She doesn't care."

"Really?" He raised his eyebrows the way he did when one of us came late to practice with some stupid excuse like he'd forgotten what day it was.

"If she cared, she'd let me play Thursday."

He didn't say anything.

"It's not fair. Everyone else gets to play except me."

"You're right, it isn't fair. But for what it's worth, I think your mom made the right decision."

"What?" I couldn't believe my ears. "If she's right, how come Jim's playing and you're coaching?"

"I can't speak for Jim. That's between him and his parents. As for me, I'm no happier about this than you are. But I can't think only of myself. I've got the team to consider. My responsibilities don't end with me. Frankly, Danny, neither do yours. I'm not gonna try to bully you into remaining on the team if you really don't want to play, but I'm not going to accept your resignation immediately either. I want you to give it more thought. You've worked hard. The team's depending on you. Timmy can't pitch the whole season alone. Neither could you. That's what it means to be part of a team, to rely on others, to expect they'll be there for you when you need them. This isn't singles tennis, it's baseball, nine men on a team, nine parts of a whole. If one of those parts is missing, the whole team suffers. You're one of those parts. Think about that."

"I've *been* thinking about it," I said. "That's all I've been thinking about."

"Well, think some more. I want to see you Saturday morning, nine o'clock. If you're playing, come suited up and ready to pitch. If not, just come and tell me so."

"Okay," I said, getting up, relieved he hadn't gotten angry, but also confused, embarrassed, and sad. I was letting him down, the one person who'd never let me down. Maybe I was making too much of one game.

100

Maybe I *was* cutting off my nose to spite my face, as Helaine said.

"I'm really sorry," I said at the door.

"Don't apologize. This is an important decision. Just give it some more thought. I'll see you Saturday."

By the time I got to the cafeteria, no one was left on line. I picked out a peanut-butter-and-jelly-sandwich and a soda—I wasn't feeling very hungry—then reached into my pocket for my lunch money. Jim's note came with it, folded so many times it was no bigger than a penny. While I waited for the cashier to give me change, I unfolded it, then laughed.

It said in angry block letters: "I can't play Thursday either." Jim had to miss the opener, too! I suddenly felt better, but only for a moment. Then I remembered I'd quit the team, and Jim was probably telling everyone about it. He was sitting with Daryl, Timmy, and Brian. I began to feel so stupid. Just because of one lousy game I was throwing the whole season away.

"Guttman!" Daryl yelled as I pocketed my change and Jim's note. He waved me over to their table. I approached slowly, trying to decide what to say. Was I quitting the team or not?

"This turkey says you're quitting the team," Daryl said, pointing his spoon at Jim.

Before I could answer, Timmy said to Daryl, "We don't need him. Bobby and I can pitch."

"Jesser? Pitch?" Jim said. "Gimme a break."

"Are you playing or not?" Daryl asked impatiently.

"I quit," I shot back.

"How come?" Brian asked.

"Because he's a jerk," Daryl replied.

Jim said to me, "I've got to miss the game, too. It's no big deal."

"It's not just that game," I said, still standing with my tray.

"I can't believe you're quitting." Daryl

turned his back on me. "That really stinks."

I was surprised that he cared, but I felt like punching him for making me feel so small.

"How would you like it if the first game was on Christmas?" I asked.

"That's really stupid," Daryl shot back over his shoulder. "No one plays baseball in December."

"What if they did?"

"I wouldn't quit the team, I know that."

"Sit down and eat your lunch," Jim said.

"I'm sitting over there," I said, spotting a table that had just emptied. I sat down alone and took a bite of my sandwich, but it tasted like sand. I could barely swallow it. I kept my eyes away from Jim's table, but after a minute he picked up his tray and joined me.

"You're acting really weird today," he said.

"So are you," I said stupidly. "I thought your parents were letting you play."

"Yeah, well, I was wrong," he grumbled.

103

"What happened?"

"They thought the first seder was Friday night. I didn't say anything, figuring by the time they found out it was Thursday, they'd have to let me play because it would be too late to tell Coach I couldn't."

"How'd they find out?"

"I opened my big trap and said you wouldn't be pitching." He kicked the table leg and muttered, "Rats!"

"So why didn't you try to make them feel guilty about it?" I asked with a smirk, repeating the advice he'd given me.

"Because it's impossible to make *both* of them feel guilty. But at least *I'm* not quitting the team."

"It's not just the seder," I said, trying to understand what it was that was making me do something everyone else thought was crazy.

"What is it, then?"

"I don't know. My mom, I guess, my dad, lots of stuff."

"Cohen, you coming?" Daryl asked, standing by the table and holding his tray.

"In a minute," Jim said. "Wanna play softball?" he asked me.

"Nah."

"Don't quit," he said, getting up. "We've got to stick together." Then he left the cafeteria.

What was that sound? I wondered, waking gradually from my dreams Thursday morning. I'd been standing on a pitcher's mound so high I was afraid of falling off, while juggling something that kept disappearing each time I tossed it into the air. I finally opened my eyes, dropped my legs over the side of the bed, and shuffled to the window. When I lifted the shade, the window was all wet.

"Yes!" I shouted, instantly awake. It was

raining! Why hadn't I thought of that? All it had to do was rain all day, and the game would be postponed. Then I could go to the seder *and* play in the opener! I couldn't believe it. All my worrying, all my anger and stewing had been a stupid waste of time. It was raining! God was on my side. He wanted me to play.

"Oh, thank you, God, thank you!" I murmured at the window. Where was my Haggadah? I needed to practice my Hebrew and review the Four Questions. I looked at the clock: 7:15. I couldn't wait to see Jim and share the good news. We'd both be able to play. I wanted to call Coach. It was raining! What a beautiful day.

"You're looking awfully chipper this morning," Mom said as I entered the kitchen. She stood at the counter, sipping coffee, all dressed for work, her briefcase and an umbrella leaning against the back door. I gave her a hug.

"What's that for?" she asked, smiling. "I thought I was still in the doghouse."

"It's raining."

"I noticed," she replied. "And I've got two meetings out of the office."

"They'll have to postpone the game."

"Aha!"

"I can go to the seder and not miss the opener."

"Does this mean you're back on the team?"

"Yeah, I guess," I said, suddenly feeling a little foolish. I wondered what Jim and the others would say when I told them. Daryl would call me a jerk. But Coach would be pleased. Or maybe not.

In an instant all my happiness drained away.

"What's the matter?" Mom asked, seeing the change on my face.

"I never should have told Coach I was quitting."

"He'll understand. Just tell him you gave it a lot of thought and changed your mind," Mom suggested.

"But he'll never trust me again."

"Oh, I think he will," she said with a

smile. "You didn't actually quit, you just talked about it."

"I missed practice. I let him down," I said sullenly.

"No, you didn't. You haven't even played your first game yet."

"But you didn't see his face when I told him." That puzzled look came back to my mind. It was as though he'd suddenly realized he'd been wrong about me.

"I'm sure Coach Resnick has had a lot of experience dealing with this sort of thing. It's just preseason jitters. I wouldn't worry about it. Go talk to him before school. You'll feel better." She washed out her coffee mug and headed upstairs to get Ali ready for day care. "Please finish up the cereal and have some toast. We've got to get rid of all the bread by tonight." Three boxes of matzah stood on the counter beside the refrigerator.

I wasn't hungry. How could Coach treat me the way he had before if he was always thinking I might quit on him? He was probably already planning my replacement, spending extra time with Timmy or Bobby.

He had to. He was the coach. He had the team to consider.

I ate a few spoonfuls of cereal and half a piece of bread, my stomach feeling queasy.

"You okay?" Mom asked as we drove to school. "You look a little pale." She reached over and felt my forehead. The rain was falling so hard we could barely see. Ali sat strapped in her car seat, drawing on the fogged-up window.

"I feel nauseous," I said.

"Just nerves. You'll be fine as soon as you speak to Coach."

The rain drummed on the roof. All the cars had their headlights on. "What a miserable day," Mom muttered. When we pulled up to school, she told me to put on my hood. "If it's still pouring at three, I'll be waiting for you right here." She leaned over and kissed my cheek. "Cheer up, kiddo. It's raining, remember?"

I tried to feel happy about that but couldn't. I ran into school, wishing I'd kept my mouth shut. I'd been so busy feeling sorry for myself I hadn't realized how dumb I was acting. The halls were still empty. On rainy days everyone came late. I dropped my books and raincoat in my locker and walked down the hall to the gym. Coach's office was empty. I waited around while the first buses arrived. Fifty kids suddenly burst into the hallway, shouting and running, water dripping from their jackets, their matted hair, their sneakers. Daryl and Timmy passed without saying hello, pretending they hadn't seen me.

The first bell rang. I walked down the hall toward the teachers' parking lot, hoping to see Coach drive up, then ran back to his office to make sure he hadn't come in another way. He hadn't. I started to scribble a note, but then the second bell rang. I was late. I stuffed the paper in my pocket and ran to class. Jim's desk was empty, as were several other desks. Mrs. Baron was writing math problems on the board.

"Settle down, class," she said. "The second bell has rung."

Jim came running in, his shoes untied, shirttail out, his hair dripping wet.

"What happened to you?" I asked as he dropped his wet books on his desk.

"We got a flat about a block from home. I ran practically the whole way."

"Jim! Danny!" Mrs. Baron snapped. "Everyone take out a clean sheet of paper and begin solving the equations on the board."

"Is this a quiz?" Jim asked.

"Yes, it is," she replied.

"You didn't say anything about a quiz yesterday."

"I wanted to surprise you," she said. "No more talking. You've got ten minutes."

"Ten minutes!" Jim complained.

"Nine," Mrs. Baron said, checking her watch.

Jim muttered, "She's so mean."

I copied the first problem and began to solve it. It was easy.

"No game today," Jim whispered. When I looked at him, he pointed to the window with his chin.

"Yeah, I know." I turned back to my work.

"So you can play," he said.

"Yeah, I guess. You too."

"Aren't you glad?"

"Jim Cohen! Come up here, please." Jim left his seat and shuffled to the front of the room. Mrs. Baron sat him in an empty desk beside her. "Seven minutes," she called out. I turned back to the remaining problems, finishing them with three minutes to spare.

As Mrs. Baron collected our papers, the lights flickered. Then suddenly the room shook with the crash of thunder. For the next several minutes the sky flickered with flashes of lightning. Rain splashed against our windows as though someone had turned a hose on them. The wind whipped the trees. The sky grew so dark we could see our reflections in the glass.

We opened our social studies books and began reading silently. Every few minutes I looked out at the storm. Gradually the thunder grew fainter. The windows stopped reflecting the classroom; the rain eased.

"Please don't stop," I muttered. Half an hour later a shaft of sunlight broke through the clouds, cutting across the blackboard.

I groaned. Mrs. Baron frowned at me. By the time we went to gym, the sky had turned bright blue. Outside, every wet surface was steaming, the asphalt, the hoods of cars, even the grass. The sun seemed to be pulling the water right out of the ground.

"I can't believe this," Jim complained. "Why couldn't it have rained at least until this afternoon? It never rains when you want it to. This really stinks."

"It could rain later," I said.

"No way. There isn't a cloud in the sky."

It serves me right, I thought. I was ready to quit the team, so why should I get to play the first game? I was being punished and almost felt better for it. I could tell Coach I wasn't quitting, and it wasn't because I was getting to play the opener but because I realized how much he'd done for me.

When we reached the gym, Coach was waiting by the door. "Outside, everyone!" he called. I wanted to speak with him, but before I could, Jim asked, "Is the game still on?"

"Looks that way," Coach replied.

"Rats!"

I opened my mouth to speak, but Coach suddenly shouted, "Ladies and gentlemen, outside, please. On the double." He seemed annoyed about something. He jogged out the door and down to the track, barking at us to follow. When we'd all assembled, he sent us on sprints around the track, then divided us into two teams for soccer. He dismissed us when the lunch bell rang, but I hung back, telling Jim I'd meet him in the cafeteria.

"Hurry up. This is the last good lunch we'll be able to eat for a week," he said. "After this it's peanut butter and jelly on matzah."

I ran after Coach as he walked back to the gym carrying a soccer ball under each arm.

"Can I talk with you a minute?" I asked.

"I'm late for a meeting." He barely looked at me. "Can it wait until after school?"

"Sure," I said, dropping back and feeling like he'd just told me to get lost. Helaine was right: I had cut off my nose to spite my face.

I didn't go to see Coach after school. I couldn't face him. What was the point? I wasn't going to play anymore, not because I didn't want to but because he didn't want me on the team. If I came back, he'd probably just sit me on the bench all season. I decided to write him a letter and leave it on his desk, apologizing and explaining. When I got home, I went up to my room, shut my door, and took out a piece of paper and a pen. Then I stared out the window, trying to decide how to say it. A robin was poking his beak into the grass, hunting worms. Somewhere nearby kids were shouting. It couldn't have been a more perfect afternoon for baseball.

Mom poked her head into my room. "Is the game on?"

"Yeah."

"Sorry." She looked at me a long moment.

"I feel so stupid," I said suddenly.

"Why?"

"I made this whole thing into a big mess. Now Coach doesn't trust me anymore."

"Oh, come on."

"He wouldn't even speak to me after gym this morning."

"Really?"

"He said he had a meeting."

"Then he probably did," she said, looking relieved.

"But he was angry at me. I could tell."

"He's got no reason to be angry. Just tell him you've decided to play."

"I can't."

"Why not?"

"I just can't."

"Because you think he's mad at you?"

I nodded.

"You face me all the time when you *know* I'm mad at you." She laughed.

"That's different. You're my mother."

"Lucky me." She noticed the stationery on my desk. "Are you writing to him?"

"Yeah. But I don't know what to say."

"Dear Coach Resnick," she began. "I'm sorry if I caused you any trouble. I'm grateful for all the help you've given me, and I'm looking forward to playing the rest of the season. My mom says she hopes that next year no one will schedule games on Passover. She also promises to come and root for us whenever she can."

"I'm not gonna say that."

"Which part?" she asked.

"The whole thing."

"Why not?"

"That's not what I want to say."

121

"Well, you've got until about four-thirty to put it in your own words. Then you have to get dressed for Ellen's. It's beautiful out. Why don't you think about this in the garden?"

"I don't want to be outside," I said, moping.

"Oh, please, Danny, no more moodiness. This has been going on for too long."

"None of this would have happened if you'd let me play."

"You think you'd feel right out there when all the other Jewish kids were at their seders?" she asked.

"Oh, I don't know," I snapped.

"I don't think you would," she said. "Sandy didn't."

At four-thirty Mom took Ali upstairs to dress her for the seder. Before going inside she told me, "I've put your sweater and dress pants on the bed." I lay in the grass under the old crab apple tree, staring up through the white blossoms. Every time the wind blew, a cloud of petals rained down on me. The game would be starting in half an hour. Soon they'd all be sitting around Coach, getting last-minute instructions while Mr. Duffy checked to make sure the bases were secure. Daryl would pound his mitt nervously with his fist; Timmy would keep swinging his arm over his head, trying to keep it loose. Then the bus from Ryewood would arrive. Through the closed doors the team would be chanting something. I felt sudden butterflies in my stomach just thinking about it. Every time the other team showed up or we pulled up to a strange field, I felt my arms go limp. Jim usually mumbled under his breath, "They think they're so cool, but we're gonna slaughter 'em." That usually got my strength back.

"Come on, Danny, I don't want to be late," Mom called from Ali's window.

"Coming," I said, pushing myself up from the grass. When I reached the top of the stairs, Ali ran out to meet me.

"New sues," she said, pointing down at her feet. She was wearing shiny black ones with little black bows.

"They look real nice," I told her.

She patted her chest with both hands and said, "Dress like Mommy."

"Doesn't she look adorable?" Mom asked. They were wearing matching blue dresses. Mom had even managed to pin a flowered barrette into Ali's delicate hair, but Ali kept yanking it out.

"Off," she said, handing it to Mom.

"It looks so pretty, sweetheart. Leave it in." Mom tried to pin it back in place, but Ali shook her head.

"They're probably warming up right now," I said, wanting to make Mom feel a little guilty.

"Who?" she asked.

"You know."

"No, I don't. Ellen?" she asked with a puzzled look.

"The team!" I said.

"Oh, yes, the team. How could I forget? I hope you're not going to spend the whole night moping about it. This is supposed to be a celebration."

"I can't help it."

"Well, try."

Half an hour later we pulled into Ellen's driveway. There were already five cars ahead of us. I noticed Arthur's Porsche and a small red station wagon that looked familiar. Mom was watching me, half-smiling. Something was up, but I didn't know what. Ellen came out to the driveway as Mom lifted Ali from the car.

"Aren't you the most precious china doll," she said, giving Ali a kiss. "Matching outfits! If that isn't the cutest. And you, Master Guttman! Don't you look dapper."

"Quite a departure from the usual torn jeans and dirty sneakers, wouldn't you say?" Mom said proudly.

Ali toddled ahead in search of Ellen's cat, calling out, "Boots, Boots!"

"He's wandered off, sweetie," Ellen called after her. "Seems to happen to all the men in my life."

We walked around back to where several

guests were standing around talking, some on the terrace, others beside the pool. Ellen's daughters, Tracy and Samantha, were offering the guests hors d'oeuvres on tiny matzah crackers. The sun was just beginning to drop behind the trees, turning the buds golden. Yellow tulips and daffodils had sprung up around the pool since our visit last Saturday.

"The garden looks beautiful," Mom said.

"It ought to, for what my gardener charges," Ellen replied.

Arthur broke away from a group of guests and joined us. He kissed Mom's cheek, leaned over and kissed the top of Ali's head, then shook my hand, squeezing it too hard. "How's the arm?" he asked.

"Wrong question," Ellen said before I could reply.

"Oh, yes, I forgot." Arthur pressed his lips together. "The game."

I hated their paying so much attention to me.

"Will there be a rematch later in the season?" Ellen asked.

"If Danny doesn't miss any more practices," a familiar voice said.

From out of the knot of guests standing by the pool Coach Resnick suddenly appeared. My mouth fell open. Ellen and Mom laughed.

"Coach!" I cried.

"Happy Pesach, Co-captain," he said, shaking my hand. We'd never shaken hands before. I'd also never seen him dressed in anything but shorts or sweatpants. Except for his crew cut, he looked like all the other parents.

"What, why, I mean...how come you're here?" I asked, all flustered. From the smile on his face I figured if he had been angry with me, he wasn't anymore.

"Marty and I go waaaay back," Ellen said, putting her arm through his.

"Brooklyn, Sheepshead Bay," Coach added.

"No kidding," Arthur said. "That was my old stomping ground."

"When I heard about your dilemma," Ellen said to me, "I decided to see if my old

buddy was free to join us. I thought that might help ease the pain. Well, *voilà*. Here he is."

"But what about the game?" I asked Coach.

"Mr. Duffy is coaching tonight."

"But I thought—"

"So did I," he interrupted. "It wasn't an easy decision. I wanted to be with the team, but I also wanted to be here."

"You did?"

He laughed. "I guess I didn't care much for seders when I was your age either, but the older I got, the more important they became. Spring just doesn't feel like spring without them."

"Not to me."

"It may someday. And then you'll look back and thank your mom for this," Coach replied.

Ellen, Mom, and Arthur drifted away.

"You're not angry with me?" I asked after a moment.

"Why should I be?"

"For wanting to quit the team."

"You still want to?"

I shook my head. "Nope."

"What changed your mind?" he asked, helping himself to one of Samantha's hors d'oeuvres.

"Lots of things."

"Like what?"

There were so many reasons: the team, his help, the game. But all I said was, "I love baseball."

He smiled. "Me too."

"And what you said about letting the team down. It wasn't fair to them."

"I didn't say it wasn't *fair*," he explained, "just that they had to be considered."

"I wish I'd known you were gonna be here," I said, suddenly feeling so relieved. "It would have made things a lot easier."

"You're right. It was a mistake. I should have made up my mind much sooner." He looked thoughtful. "You helped me with that, you know."

"I did?"

"When I was in the minors, I never

played on Jewish holidays. It just didn't seem right. We had other pitchers, lots of them. But being coach is different. I didn't have only myself to consider but all you guys. From the moment I got the schedule until you walked into my office, I told myself I owed it to all of you to coach. But after our talk Tuesday I realized just how important it was for me to be here. I would not have been a good coach today."

A little boy about Ali's age wandered over and grabbed hold of Coach's pant leg. "I'd like you to meet someone," Coach said, picking the boy up in his arms and kissing his cheek. "This is my son, Max."

"Hi, Max," I said, feeling my stomach suddenly sink. Coach had never mentioned he had a son.

"Say hi to Danny," Coach said.

"Hi," Max replied in a tiny, piping voice.

"He's got a terrific little arm," Coach said proudly. "You're gonna be a pitcher just like Danny, right?"

Max replied by pretending to throw a ball, hitting his father in the shoulder.

"Ow," Coach kidded. "Not so hard."

"There you are," a woman's voice said. It was Coach's wife. I'd seen her occasionally after school. Her hair was almost as short as Coach's.

"Lisa, you know Danny," Coach said, putting his arm around her. They reminded me of a picture in our den of Dad holding me when I was about Max's age and Mom standing beside us. For a moment I wished I was that age again.

"Ellen wants to know how good your Hebrew is," she said to her husband.

"Tell her, not very."

From down by the pool Ellen announced, "Sun's beginning to set. Shall we step inside and begin the festivities?"

Coach took his family into the dining room while I waited for Mom and Ali to come up from the pool. In the dying light I suddenly wished Dad was there.

When we had all assembled around Ellen's long dining room table, she lit the holiday candles, two tall white tapers in shiny silver candlesticks, and asked us to join her in saying the Hebrew prayer welcoming the holiday. Then she turned to Arthur, who was sitting at the opposite end of the table, and said, "It's all yours, Art."

Arthur removed small reading glasses from his shirt pocket, set them on the end of his nose, and picked up the Haggadah.

"My Hebrew's a little rusty," he apologized, "so please bear with me."

Then he began to read the first prayers and tell the story of the Exodus from Egypt, how the Jews had been slaves there for hundreds of years, building ancient cities for the pharaohs, and how God one day ordered Moses to go before Pharaoh and demand that he "let my people go," but Pharaoh refused. Then God sent the ten plagues, turning water to blood, covering everything with frogs and lice, destroying Egyptian crops with hailstorms and locusts, and finally killing all the Egyptian firstborn children. That's when God ordered Moses to tell all the Jews to mark their doors with the blood of a ram, so that the angel of death would *pass over* every Jewish door and spare those inside.

As he told the story of the parting of the Red Sea and of the miracle of manna in the desert, we ate the special holiday foods that were supposed to remind us of life in ancient Egypt.

"This is the matzah the fleeing Israelites

baked on stones and carried on their backs in place of bread," Arthur explained, holding it up for all to see. Then, pointing to the seder plate, he said, "We eat this bitter horseradish root and dip parsley into salt water to remind us of the bitterness and tears of slavery. The sweet apples and raisins remind us of the mortar and bricks used to build Egypt's ancient cities, and the egg symbolizes spring and rebirth."

Every few minutes we raised our wineglasses (all the kids got grape juice instead) for yet another blessing over the "fruit of the vine." When it came time to ask the first of the Four Questions, Arthur looked over the top of his glasses at me and asked, "Danny, would you care to continue on the bottom of page twenty-nine?"

I could feel everyone's eyes on me, especially Coach's. It was almost like stepping onto the mound with two outs and the bases loaded. The pitches had to be perfect or the game would be lost. You didn't get a second chance. I didn't want to make a mistake. I looked quickly over the Hebrew, then lifted my eyes and scanned the long table. Everyone was smiling at me.

"Ma nish-ta-na ha-lai-lah ha-zeh mi-kol ha-lei-lot." *Why is this night different from all other nights?* The words just spilled out of me like a well-rehearsed speech. I let my eyes wander over the table as I spoke them, feeling very important and wishing Dad were there to see me. The other three questions, about why we eat matzah and bitter herbs and dine like princes, followed. I didn't have to look down at the Haggadah. The words were there, on the tip of my tongue, like four good fastballs crossing the plate, each one a strike. Coach smiled at me and winked as I spoke. Ellen's uncle Sid, a round man with a completely bald head, nodded, mouthing the words along with me, and Mom patted my knee. When I finished, Arthur said, "That was beautiful, Danny."

Mom leaned over and kissed my cheek. "I'm proud of you," she whispered. I couldn't help smiling.

"You know why this night is different?" Uncle Sid asked, looking at me. Before I could answer, he said, "Because at this very moment, Jews all over the world are doing exactly the same thing. Can you feel it? It's like Christmas Eve to the Gentiles. There are all kinds of Jews in this world, but when it comes to Passover, something special, something they can't escape, makes them search out a seder, sit down together, and remember. It's in the blood."

I thought of Dad all the way across the Atlantic at a seder in Italy, and suddenly he didn't seem so far away.

When Ali grew restless, Mom released her from her seat and let her run around the dining room. Max demanded the same freedom and, as soon as his feet hit the floor, began chasing her. Then he discovered the forest of legs under the table, crawled in among our shoes, and eventually fell asleep. We woke him when it was time to hunt for the *afikoman,* the hidden matzah. Arthur had placed two pieces within easy view for Max and Ali, and more difficult ones for Tracy, Samantha, and me. "According to tradition," Arthur explained, sitting back and removing his glasses, "we can't continue the seder until you kids find the matzah. In other words, our future is in your hands."

"I never thought of that," Uncle Sid remarked.

"Whoever finds the *afikoman* gets a special prize," Ellen announced, holding five brightly wrapped gifts in her hands.

"I think you're going to like yours," Mom said to me. She winked at Arthur.

Ali reached for one, saying, "Present," and Max immediately imitated her, both trying to climb onto Ellen's lap.

"You have to find the matzah first," Ellen said. But they didn't seem to understand. So she broke off a piece from the matzah on her plate and pretended to hide it behind her. They circled around her chair. Ali said, "See it!"

"Now go find the other ones."

Lisa turned Max in the direction of the living room and said, "Look by the sofa." Max toddled off, followed by Ali. Tracy and

Samantha went looking as well.

Ali discovered her *afikoman* in a candy dish and cried, "Matzah!" Max tried to take it from her, crumbling it into tiny bits. Lisa separated them and sent Max in search of his own piece, steering him toward the piano, where it lay upon the keys. Ellen handed them their gifts, which they tore open, scattering crayons over the carpet. Ellen's daughters found their matzah and received matching silver rings.

I stooped down and peered under tables and chairs, looked behind all the picture frames on the piano, and checked behind the drapes. Ellen's eyes glinted with pleasure. "Need help?" she asked.

"Nope."

I scanned the bookshelves, looked behind pillows and under carpets. When I glanced back at Ellen, she was jerking her head from side to side, showing everyone where she had hidden the *afikoman*. I picked up the direction of her nod and hurried to the far end of the room, where dozens of old family photographs hung on the wall.

Among them was an old marriage certificate, a *ketubah,* written in Hebrew with faded but once colorful vines and birds decorating the borders. There, perched on the top of the frame, stood the missing piece of matzah. As I reached up for it, everyone clapped.

"Congratulations!" Ellen said, handing me the remaining gift, a small box about the size of a baseball.

"Before you open it," Mom said, "I want you to guess what's inside."

"Crayons?" I replied.

"We figured you'd outgrown them," she said.

"A tiny TV?"

"Wishful thinking."

"Computer disks."

"Not a bad guess, but nope."

"Season tickets to the Yankees."

"Close," Mom said, raising her eyebrows.

So it was a baseball after all, I realized, disappointed. I already had several.

"A baseball," I declared flatly.

"That's right!" she announced, looking across the table at Arthur. "But not just any baseball. Open it."

Not just any baseball! I ripped off the paper and opened the box. Inside was a leather hardball yellow with age, names written all over it: Roy Campanella, Gil Hodges, Pee Wee Reese, Jackie Robinson. It took me a minute to realize what I was holding.

"Oh, my God!" I cried. "The Brooklyn Dodgers!"

"Nineteen fifty-six," Arthur announced.

"The whole team?" I asked, turning the ball over slowly, reading each name.

"Yup. They won the pennant that year but lost to the Yanks in seven."

"That must be worth a fortune!" Uncle Sid said.

"It *is* valuable," Arthur replied, "but it's in good hands." He came over next to me. "Look at this—Don Newcombe." He pointed to a name scribbled on the ball.

"Wow! He won the Cy Young Award," I

said, turning to Mom, "just like Sandy Koufax."

"Also MVP that year," Coach added, looking over my shoulder.

"Most Valuable Player," I explained.

"And here." Arthur pointed. "Duke Snider—he led the league in home runs that year."

"May I see it a moment?" Coach asked. He didn't want to merely read the names; he wanted to feel the weight of the ball, the smoothness of the old leather, the carefully sewn seams. "They don't make them like this anymore," he said wistfully, handing it back to me. "What a beauty! You're a lucky guy."

I gently cupped both hands around it, wishing I were on the mound at that moment.

"You like it?" Mom asked.

"Like it? I love it!" I cried.

And then, before I knew what I was doing, I threw my arms around Arthur and hugged him as though he were Dad. I could feel his surprise in the way his arms hesitated a moment before coming down on my shoulders, but then he returned my hug and said, "I thought you'd appreciate it."

"Thanks!" I said, releasing him.

"It was my most treasured possession as a kid," Arthur explained, "not because it was valuable—I didn't think of those things then—but because those guys were my heroes. I wanted to be a pitcher just like you when I was your age."

I remembered how well he threw the apple against the tree in Ellen's garden.

Uncle Sid put on his glasses and asked to see the ball, then passed it to his wife. "You take good care of it," he said to me.

"I will," I insisted, watching it move around the table.

"I kept it with me all through college," Arthur explained, "not because I still hoped to make the majors—I'd long since given up that dream—but to remind me of how passionately I'd wanted to become something. You've got that dream, Danny. It may change, but I hope you'll always find within you that same drive to excel, whatever you choose to do."

Mom reached over and squeezed Arthur's hand. Then Ellen turned to Coach and said, "Does everyone here know that you played baseball professionally?"

"Not in the majors," he explained modestly.

"But you would have," I insisted, "if you hadn't hurt your arm."

"I don't know," he replied. "The competition was pretty stiff."

Lisa slipped her arm through his. "My husband was being scouted by the Phillies."

"Really!" Arthur said, impressed.

"Everyone back to your seats," Ellen ordered. "The seder is not over yet."

"She's worse than Pharaoh," Uncle Sid declared, "and I knew him personally."

"Much worse," Ellen agreed. "I have no intention of letting my people go free, not until you've eaten every last matzah ball, gefilte fish, and macaroon."

Arthur found his place in the Haggadah, and we finished the seder, reciting the last blessings, taking a final sip from our wine-glasses, and ending, as we did every year, with a wish for universal peace by declaring, "Next year in Jerusalem."

Uncle Sid groaned as he pushed his chair back from the table. "I haven't eaten this much since your Bat Mitzvah," he told Ellen. Then he turned to Arthur and congratulated him on leading a wonderful seder. "Every year I think to myself, Here we go again, the same old story, but every year it's different, and every year I learn something new."

Arthur winked at me. "I'm glad you enjoyed it."

I held the baseball, reading all the names. I couldn't wait to show it to Jim.

"So?" Mom asked.

"This is great," I said, palming the ball. "Wait till the guys see it. They're gonna be so jealous. Thanks, Arthur." I shook his hand, feeling as though I had crossed a bridge, leaving behind the old angry me.

"You're very welcome." He squeezed my

forearm. "I can't think of anyone who deserves it more. Maybe it'll bring you good luck this season."

I suddenly realized I hadn't thought about the opening game in hours. "I guess the game's over by now," I said to Coach.

He looked at his watch. "Should be."

"I wonder how we did."

"Whatever happened, we've got the whole season ahead of us. You ready to start Saturday?"

"You bet."

We didn't just lose the opener, we got killed. When I got to school the next morning, Timmy and Brian were standing beside my locker.

"It wasn't even close," Timmy said, rubbing his elbow. "They creamed us. A three-run homer *and* a grand slam!"

"Final score?" I asked.

"Twelve to two," Brian answered sullenly.

"Twelve to two!"

"Worst game of my life," Timmy admitted. "Duffy pulled me after four innings."

"Who'd he put in? Jesser?"

"He was out sick."

"So who pitched?"

"Deagan."

"Daryl!"

"For one inning. Then Brown and Stokes."

"They can't pitch."

"No kidding." Timmy shook his head. "It was awful. We really could have used you."

I felt a sudden tingling in my chest. It was the first time Timmy had ever said anything nice about my pitching.

"Thanks. I wanted to be there, but..." I was about to say, "My mom wouldn't let me play," but said instead, "It's Passover."

"Yeah, I know," he replied. "My mom told me all about it. You had a special meal or something?"

"A seder."

"Can you play Saturday?"

"Yup." I couldn't wait to get back on the mound.

"And Coach?"

"He'll be there. You'd have pitched better with him coaching. I'm terrible when he's out."

"I don't know," Timmy said. "Nothing felt right. It was like we'd all forgotten how to play baseball. You should have seen the errors at second. Coach is gonna kill us when he finds out."

We weren't scheduled to practice that afternoon, but Coach sent a note around at lunch saying he wanted to see everyone for five minutes after school.

"Here it comes," Brian said. The whole team was sitting around one long table, replaying the game. "He's gonna explode."

"It's his fault," Daryl said, throwing back his shoulders. "He should have been there. Duffy can't coach."

"He would have been there if the league hadn't scheduled the game on Passover," I replied in Coach's defense. "It's an important holiday."

"Whatever!" Daryl snapped. "We looked like complete turkeys out there."

When everyone had finished eating, I said, "You guys wanna see something really awesome?" Then I took out Arthur's gift and passed it around. "The whole Brooklyn Dodgers team signed it in 1956."

"'Fifty-six! That's when my dad was born," Timmy said. "That's really old!"

"Where'd you get it?" Matty asked.

"Friend of the family," I said, feeling lucky I knew Arthur.

Brian offered to trade his twelve-speed for it. Eddie asked if he could copy down all the names. Daryl said it was probably a fake.

At three o'clock all of us gathered in Coach's office. He didn't look angry, and as soon as he began talking, we knew he wasn't.

"First of all, I want to apologize to all of you for what happened yesterday. I'm sorry I wasn't there. It would have been better to forfeit the game than to play with half a team. It wasn't fair to you or Coach Duffy. And it wasn't fair to Ryewood either. They didn't get the game they deserved. I've put in a call to their coach to see if we can schedule a rematch. It won't count in the standings, but at least it'll be a fair fight."

Timmy and Brian exchanged wide-eyed looks of relief.

"That doesn't mean we don't have a lot of work to do. I understand there were lots of mental errors out there, silly mistakes, throws to wrong bases. You've got to play with your head as well as your body. In any case, don't measure yourselves by what happened yesterday. It's easy to get demoralized when you're not playing with a full team."

He rose to dismiss us. "Tomorrow morning, 9:00 A.M. against the Wolverines. You're gonna have to play your best game. They're a tough team. Gentlemen, get a good night's sleep."

"So, did the Hornets win yesterday?" Mom asked over dinner.

"We got slaughtered," I said. Ali sat in her high chair, feeding herself.

"You coming to the game tomorrow?" I asked Mom.

"What time?"

"Nine."

Mom groaned.

"Never mind," I said, trying to act as though I didn't care.

"Is it okay if I arrive a little late?"

"Coach said I'm starting."

"Okay, I'll shoot for nine," she said with a sigh.

"If you're too tired, that's okay," I insisted.

Mom leaned over and kissed my cheek.

"Kiss," Ali said, smacking her lips. Mom kissed her, too.

"I'm sorry I gave you such a hard time about the seder," I said.

"Did you enjoy it?"

"Yeah," I admitted. "It was fun. Arthur was great."

"He was very impressed with your Hebrew."

153

"Are you two going out tonight?"

"Just to a movie," she said, looking at her watch. "Helaine should be here soon."

"Lane come?" Ali asked.

"Any minute."

When the phone rang, I knew from the sound of Mom's voice it was Dad. She always got very stiff and formal when she spoke to him. I watched her pace back and forth across the kitchen.

"Yes, very nice, and yours?... He did, in Hebrew, perfectly." She winked at me. "He's right here." She held the phone out to me.

"Dad?"

"Happy Passover," he said. His voice was so clear he sounded as if he was calling from next door.

"Where are you?" I asked.

"Still in Milan. We were just about to turn in for the night, and I thought I'd give my boy a call. How was your seder?"

"Okay. When are you coming home?" I suddenly felt a great need to hug him.

"Week from Sunday. Everything okay?"

Tears sprang to my eyes. "Yeah, it's just that I miss you."

"I miss you too, big guy," he replied. "Your mother says you read the Hebrew beautifully. I'm proud of you."

"Thanks." I felt awkward speaking to him with Mom standing there.

"We've got a date at Yankee Stadium when I get back, remember?"

"Yup. Wanna speak to Ali?" I needed to get off the phone and be alone.

"In a minute. You sure you're okay?"

"Yeah, I'm fine. Hurry back." I normally would have told him to say hello to Marie for me, but with Mom there I decided not to mention her.

"See you soon," he said, still sounding concerned.

I handed the phone to Ali, then ran upstairs and sat at my desk, turning Arthur's baseball around in my hands, feeling suddenly guilty, as though I'd somehow betrayed Dad by accepting it.

The next day we lost to the Wolverines by two. Coach started me but put Timmy in after three innings. By that time I'd given up six hits, four walks, and two runs. I just couldn't find my fastball or the inside edge of the plate. I was glad Mom wasn't there to see it. By the time she arrived, Timmy was on the mound. After the game, Coach concentrated on our few successes, like the double play in the sixth and Jim's steal of third. "We got off to a rocky start,"

he said, "but got better every inning."

We won our next game, beating the Tigers in eleven innings on an error by their shortstop, and then began to get our confidence back. By the middle of the season it felt like we couldn't lose. Coach started me every other game, letting me pitch four, five, sometimes six innings. Timmy pitched the rest, with Bobby coming in whenever we had a strong lead. Word got around school that we were having our best season ever, and lots of kids began showing up to cheer us on. We kept pressing Coach to set up a rematch with Ryewood, but he said their coach couldn't find time in their schedule.

"They're chicken," Jim declared as we sat in the grass after practice one afternoon near the end of the regular season. The days were getting longer and hotter. The end of school was two weeks away. Summer was coming.

"You'll just have to live with it for now," Coach replied. "Keep playing as well as you've been playing, and we may just meet them in the play-offs. They're nine and one." We'd won eight and lost two.

Dad returned home a week after Passover but, instead of taking me to Yankee Stadium as he'd promised, had to leave again immediately for a trial in Los Angeles. It wasn't his fault—the court moved up the trial date. He called me once a week from California and reminded me that he hadn't forgotten his promise; it would just have to wait until after the trial. I didn't really mind. I was busy writing my big end-of-the-year book report, practicing with the team, and swimming at the town pool. Most nights, after finishing my homework, I lay on the carpet in the den, watching the Yankees or the Mets. Sometimes Mom and Arthur joined me.

Early one Friday evening in June, I came home after practice and found Mom getting ready to go out. "You gonna be late tonight?" I asked.

"Why? Are you planning a wild party or something?"

"Our championship game's tomorrow, 9:00 A.M.," I said, already feeling disappointed. She'd never make it if she stayed out after midnight.

"Ryewood, right?" Mom said, surprising me.

"Right!" We'd won our first two play-off games, beating both the Wolverines and the Tigers.

"I'll be there," she said. "Baseball's my life."

"Oh, sure."

"My alarm's already set. Arthur's coming, too."

"Really?" I'd finally get to show them how much better I'd gotten. "What's for dinner?"

"Hot dogs, pretzels, peanuts, and beer," she said with a mischievous smile.

"What?"

"How'd you like to watch the Yankees play the Orioles?"

"On TV?"

"At Yankee Stadium, you ninny."

"Tonight?"

"Arthur's got three tickets."

"You're kidding!"

"Would I kid you about something that important?"

Two hours later the three of us were sitting behind first base, almost close enough to touch the runners as they raced to the bag, kicking up dirt. The infield grass was so green it looked spray-painted. Mom sat on my right, Arthur on my left. Music and advertisements blared from the huge centerfield screen.

"Hot dog?" Arthur shouted at us as a vendor walked by. We nodded and eventually were stuffing ourselves with sodas, Cracker Jacks, pretzels, peanuts, and ice-cream sandwiches. Mom watched the game carefully for the first two innings, asking the names of all the batters and pitchers, cheering whenever anyone got a hit, no matter which team, amazed by how far the outfielders could throw the ball. "I never realized it's so big," she said of the field.

It had been sunny and hot when we arrived, but gradually the sun set, the air

cooled, the lights came on, and by the fourth inning a half-moon hung above the stadium. Every few minutes the scoreboard flashed messages to the audience, getting us to clap or shout or stamp our feet, exploding with fireworks whenever the Yankees got a hit.

Between the fifth and sixth innings the scoreboard flashed the message "Karen, will you marry me? Evan."

"Look at that," Mom cried. "Somebody's proposing in the middle of Yankee Stadium."

The stadium cameras roamed over the audience, then zoomed in on a young man kneeling beside the seat of a woman covering her face with her hands. Behind her several couples holding soda cans were laughing and chanting something. When the woman finally nodded yes and threw her arms around the kneeling man, the chanting couples poured soda over their heads, and the whole stadium erupted in cheers.

Arthur looked at Mom and winked. "Not exactly my idea of romantic."

"Or mine," she agreed.

Every inning the crowd got louder and more excited. By the eighth inning, with the score tied, the whole stadium jumped to its feet with every foul tip and fly ball. By the ninth, no one was sitting. With two outs, the Orioles got to first on a walk, stole second, and scored on a double. Then the Yankees got up, put their first three men on, loading the bases, and then, one by one, struck out, three times in a row. The crowd booed and stamped and threw programs on the field in disgust, but I thought the Orioles' relief pitcher had thrown some of the best pitches I'd ever seen. I hoped to do as well against Ryewood.

I awoke the next morning with a teddy bear pressed against my face. Ali had climbed out of her crib and was standing beside my bed saying, "No sleep, Danny."

I grabbed her chubby arms and pulled her up onto the bed, then began tickling her. She giggled at first, squirming under my fingers, but suddenly declared, "No tickle!" and slid down to the floor.

"You gonna watch me pitch today?" I asked.

"No tickle," she repeated, pulling my covers to the floor.

"Hey, stop that." I yanked them back.

Mom came in wearing her bathrobe and rubbing her eyes. "Did you climb out of your crib again, you little devil?"

Ali hugged her legs.

"I guess it's time to get you a big bed." She sat at the edge of my bed and asked, "Ready for the big game?"

I stretched my arm over my head and rubbed my shoulder. "I'm ready." Coach hadn't decided who would start, but both Timmy and I would pitch.

"Did you have a good time last night?"

"It was great."

"I did, too," she declared. "So did Arthur. He's meeting me at your game."

"He better not root for Ryewood."

"If he does, I'll kick him," she promised.

The phone rang, and Mom left the room to answer it, then called to me to pick up. It was Coach.

"How's your arm?" he asked.

"Great," I said, surprised by his call.

166

"You may have a long game ahead of you."

"Am I starting?"

"And maybe finishing. Timmy's out."

"How come?" I asked.

"Just got three stitches in his index finger."

"What happened?"

"He was doing something with a jackknife, and it slipped. Jesser and Wright will back you up. See you in an hour."

When I got off the phone, I slammed my fist into my palm and said, "Yes!"

As the game got under way, Mom, Arthur, and Ali were sitting beside the Cohens in the first row of the bleachers. Helaine and Sol were right behind them, eating popcorn out of a huge bucket. Our first batter grounded out to short, the next popped up to right field, the third struck out. Their pitcher was strong. His fastball was murder. The game had barely started, and already we felt we were losing. Their captain, a big guy they called Moose, taunted us from center field. He was the one who'd hit the grand slam against Timmy during the season opener.

When I struck out my first batter, Sol yelled, "Way to go, Koufax!"

Coach, his hands cupped around his mouth, kept up a constant stream of instructions from the dugout while the rest of our team jeered at the batters. We got the next two batters out on pop flies and felt our confidence return.

My first time at bat, I lined out to third. "You'll get it by him next time, slugger!" Sol cried as I walked back to the bench.

The game remained scoreless until the fourth inning. Brian hit a double and then scored when Daryl drove a single past the shortstop. In the sixth inning, I walked the leadoff batter. As he stole second, Eddie's throw from the plate went wide, and the runner reached third standing up. The next two batters popped out to the infield. Then Moose stepped up to the plate, glaring at me, daring me to throw a strike. I wanted to throw the ball down his throat, pitch it so fast he'd never see it. I checked the runner at third, making sure he didn't take too big a lead, wound up, and hurled the ball as hard as I could. The crack of the bat was so loud I felt it in my chest. I didn't have to look to know the ball was gone. It soared over Jim's head and the right-field fence. Moose loped around the bases with a stupid grin on his face while the rest of the Rye-wood team shouted, "Moose! Moose!" and leaped all over him as he crossed the plate. I stood on the mound, my arms at my sides, feeling the blood rush to my face. When I looked at Coach, he nodded at me with his "Bear down" expression.

Jim yelled from the outfield, "That's okay, Danny, we'll get it back. Strike 'em out. You can do it."

Coach clapped his hands and shouted, "Two outs, boys. You only need one more. Let's go, Danny." I wound up and pitched. The batter popped up to second, and the inning was over, the score 2–1, Ryewood. When I came off the mound, Coach asked if I wanted to be relieved. "Bobby's warming up," he said. I looked over at Jesser pitching to Mr. Duffy.

I shook my head. "I can do it," I insisted. "I should have pitched inside to that big jerk."

"There's no disgrace in going six innings. How's the arm feel?"

"Fine." I didn't tell him that my elbow was beginning to hurt.

"Don't try to be a hero," Coach said. "If you've had enough, tell me."

But I wanted to be a hero. I wanted Mom to see how good a pitcher I was. I wanted her to take my playing as seriously as Coach did. And I wanted to impress Arthur.

"They won't score another run," I promised.

Coach slapped me on the back and sent me to the on-deck circle. I hadn't gotten a hit all game. "Everyone hits this inning," Coach called out. "Don't swing for the fences. Singles, boys. Concentrate." Then, more quietly, he observed, "Third base is playing too close to the bag. Big hole there. Try to drive it through."

I connected with the second pitch, finding another hole between first and second for an easy single. When I reached the base, I stood with one foot on the bag and looked toward the bleachers. Everyone was cheering. Mom, Arthur, and Helaine were on their feet, shouting as though I'd hit a home run. Coach called out, "Nice going, Danny! Everyone hits. Let's go, Jimmy—drive Danny to second."

Jim took two balls and a strike, then connected, bouncing the ball hard to third base. I dug in, running as fast as I could, thinking, Don't let them get the double play. And they didn't. The second baseman dropped the ball as I slid into the bag, and both Jim and I were safe. Then the Cohens were on their feet, too. Ryewood got very quiet all of a sudden, so quiet their coach had to tell them to "talk it up out there, boys. This isn't a funeral."

Mr. Duffy, coaching third base, signaled me to watch him for running instructions as Eddie stepped up to the plate. Eddie swung and missed the first pitch, let a ball go by, then took a called second strike. "Come on, Eddie," Coach called from the bench, "loosen up. Little single." Eddie nodded, his eyes fixed on the pitcher. When the ball crossed the plate, he met it, popping it over the first baseman's head. The right fielder scooped it up and threw it to first, beating out Eddie, but Jim scrambled to second and I reached third.

"Nice running," Mr. Duffy said, patting me on the back as Daryl stepped up to the plate. If we had a Moose of our own, it was Daryl, the only one on our team who could hit the ball over the fence. But he was erratic and hadn't been hitting well in the play-offs. He let the first pitch go by, a perfect strike, then swung so hard he spun around and lost his footing, falling to the side. The Ryewood infield jeered, "He can't even stand up. Easy out, easy out."

"Just meet it," Coach said.

Daryl looked angry. He let the next ball go by, a ball, then connected on the fourth pitch, sending it deep into center field. Moose was there, waiting, glove up. I crouched low at third, ready to explode off the bag. As the ball touched Moose's glove, Mr. Duffy cried, "Go, Danny! Go, go, go, go, go!" I raced for home, hearing nothing but the sound of my cleats churning up the dirt, seeing nothing but their catcher standing between me and the plate, his round padded glove reaching for the ball I knew was chasing me.

"Slide!" someone screamed. I threw my legs out in front of me and hit the dirt, skidding along the white line and crashing into the catcher, knocking him down just as the ball soared over my head.

"Safe!" the umpire yelled. The team exploded in cheers. Mom and Arthur leaped to their feet again. Helaine and Sol tossed handfuls of popcorn in the air. The bleachers erupted in shouts of "Hor-nets! Hor-nets!" The team surrounded me, slapping my back and shoulders, crying, "Way to go, Danny!" The score was tied.

The Ryewood coach walked slowly out to the mound to speak with his pitcher. The third baseman taunted Jim, shouting,

"Don't worry about Fatso. He's not going anywhere." Mr. Duffy winked at Jim.

With a full count, Matty connected, sending the ball over second base. Moose was there, scooping it up after one bounce. But then he made the kind of mental error that had lost the opener for us. Instead of throwing to first for the easy out, he saw Jim heading home, forgot there were already two outs, and fired the ball toward the plate. It never got there. The ball went wide, and Jim crossed the plate standing up. We were ahead 3–2, with Matty on second. Everyone went wild. I looked over at the bleachers and saw Ali sitting on Arthur's shoulders, wearing Helaine's empty popcorn bucket on her head. Our next batter hit the ball back to the pitcher and was thrown out at first, ending the inning.

I gave up two hits in the seventh inning—including a double by Moose—and three in the eighth, but we got the lead runner out both times, and no one scored. My elbow was really aching, but I kept it to myself, careful not to rub it while on the mound. I was determined to finish the game. When I came off the mound, Coach said, "Keep it warm." I put my Hornets windbreaker on. He knew my elbow was sore, but Bobby wasn't looking too good in warm-ups.

My last time at bat, I was so eager to get a hit that I swung wildly at the first two pitches. Coach called, "Time!" and walked over to the batter's box. "Easy, Danny," he said. "This game isn't over by a long shot. We don't need homers, just singles. This is where games are won and lost. Concentrate. Use your head, look for the holes."

I stepped back up to the plate thinking, Slow and steady, eye on the ball, just meet it. The muscles tensed in my wrists and forearms, neck and shoulders. Bat back, I thought, Feet apart. Hate that ball, hit it with your whole body. *Concentrate!* The next pitch looked good, then suddenly turned inside. I checked my swing and looked back at the umpire, praying for the right call.

"Ball," he said. "One and two."

I turned back to the pitcher. He was grinning and probably thinking, One more pitch and this batter's history. I knew the feeling. After a while you could tell when a batter had lost confidence, when he'd just watch strike three cross the plate or swing wildly at anything. I wasn't going to let that happen to me. I knew I could get a hit. I glared back at him, waiting while he checked the empty bases, rubbed his right hand across his chest, then against his leg, reached into his glove, twirled the ball around in his fingers to get the grip just right, and wound up.

That was my pitch. The crack of the bat, the vibration in my hands, the follow-through of my arms, chest, and hips— everything felt right. It's gone, I thought, racing toward first. I'd never hit a homer before. But just as it seemed about to sail over the fence, Moose's glove appeared out of nowhere and pulled it from the air.

"You were robbed!" Arthur yelled as I sulked back to the bench.

"Nice try," Coach said. "I thought you had it."

"Don't you hate that big jerk?" Jim asked, swinging two bats in the on-deck circle.

"Knock one down his throat," I replied.

Jim got to first on a walk, then stole second. But no one else hit, so we returned to the field for the last half of the ninth inning with only a one-run lead.

My wrist and shoulder were hurting by then, but I tried to ignore the pain, telling myself, All you need is three outs and it's over. I threw two warm-up pitches and could tell I was slowing down. I couldn't get any power behind the ball. Their first batter took two balls, then hit the third pitch hard, lining out to third. It was a lucky break. Matty was in perfect position. Coach shouted, "Two more, boys, two more!"

The second batter dropped one in short left field for a single. My hands began to sweat. The tying run was on base. Their next batter bunted. Eddie scooped up the ball and made the out at first, but the lead runner reached second. The crowd chanted, "One more out! One more out!"

When the third batter stepped up to the plate, I wound up and released the pitch. I never saw or heard the ball coming back at me; I only felt it smash into my chest, knocking me on my back. By the time I managed to find it underneath my leg, there were runners on first and third.

I brushed myself off, rubbed my chest, and stepped back on the mound. Mom looked ready to run out onto the field and carry me home. Eddie jogged up from the plate, his catcher's mask on top of his head.

"You okay?" he asked. I nodded and looked over at Coach. He held up his index finger. Just one more out to go.

I knew the moment the next pitch left my fingertips that it was out of control. The batter stepped back, but it hit him in the shoulder. As he jogged to first base, the rest of the Ryewood team jeered, "Pitcher's cracking!" The bases were loaded.

Coach called, "Time!" and walked out to the mound. "How bad does it hurt?" he asked. Without realizing it, I had begun to rub my elbow.

"I'm okay," I insisted.

He took my left arm in his hands and slowly kneaded it. "We don't want to lose it now."

"I can do it," I assured him.

"You've been doing it for nine innings. You deserve a rest. You've pitched a great game, the best of the season."

"I'll get the next batter out."

"It's Moose."

I looked toward the batter's box. Moose stood beside it, swinging three bats. The whole Ryewood bench was chanting, "Let's go, Moose!"

"I'm gonna strike the big jerk out!" I said.

"Can you keep it low and inside?"

"I'll try."

Coach studied me a moment, then said, "This is it," and patted me on the back. My heart was pounding. It was up to me.

Moose stepped into the batter's box. He looked almost as big as Coach. I rubbed the

ball in both hands, put my glove back on, and checked the runners. The first pitch just caught the inside corner for a called strike. My confidence flooded back. The infield was roaring at me. I aimed for the same corner again. This time Moose tipped it, fouling it back over the bleachers. "That's getting a piece of it," his coach yelled. "One more strike," Daryl cried. Everyone was on their feet. I missed the corner with the next one for a ball, and then missed it again twice more, hitting the dirt with the third one. Luckily, Eddie trapped it and held the runners. By then everyone was shouting, their team, our team, the bleachers, and the voice in my head that kept saying, *Bear down, Danny. Concentrate!*

The count was full. I glanced at Coach. His eyes were fixed on me, but he had no instructions. It was my game now. I would win it or lose it on the next pitch. Mom and Helaine shouted in unison, "You can do it, Danny!" I wiped my hands on my chest, turned the ball over in my hand, checked the runners again, then wound up and released the ball. I heard the crack and spun around to watch the ball soar deep into right field. Jim pedaled backward faster and faster, nearing the fence, then suddenly leaped into the air. He and the ball disappeared in a cloud of dust, cleats, and arms. The runners were circling the bases, headed for home. Then Jim stood up, holding the ball in the tip of his mitt.

"Batter's out!" the umpire yelled. "That's the ball game!"

Jim ran toward the infield waving the ball over his head. At second base he was swamped by the rest of the team. I ran over to join them. They turned and jumped on me, slapping my back and shouting, "Great pitching, Danny!" Then we all jumped on Coach, hanging from his neck and shoulders as he laughed and said, "Cohen, next time, two hands, please."

I tiptoed into Mom's room the next morning to tell her I was heading over to the pool. My left arm felt as though it had been hit by a car. But each time I rubbed it, I smiled at the thought of our victory.

"How does the world's greatest pitcher feel?" she asked, her voice heavy with sleep.

"Great," I said.

"Ellen invited us all for a swim," she murmured.

"The whole team's gonna be at the pool," I said. "Even Coach."

"Sounds like more fun than Ellen's," she said with a smile.

"Thanks, Mom." I kissed her cheek.

The phone rang. Mom picked up. In her throaty morning voice she said, "Uh-huh. Yup. He's right here," then handed the receiver to me. "It's Daddy," she said. I smiled. She hadn't called him "Daddy" in years.

"Hi, Dad!" I said.

"So?" he asked.

"We won!"

"*Mazel tov!* I thought of you all day yesterday. Did you pitch?"

"The whole game."

"The whole game! I'm so sorry I missed it."

"When are you coming home?"

"Tuesday."

"This Tuesday?"

"Yup. And I've got tickets for Friday night, Yanks against the Red Sox. Interested?"

"Dad!"

"Then they're yours. We're gonna take in a lot more games in the future. I'm counting on you to teach your new brother or sister all the fine points. Give Ali a kiss for me. I'll see you Tuesday night."

"I love you, Dad."

"I love you, too, kiddo."

"Want to speak to Mom again?"

"Sure."

As I handed her the phone, she covered the mouthpiece and said, "Arthur wants to take us all out tonight to celebrate."

"Yankee Stadium?" I asked.

"Someplace a little quieter, I think, and with slightly better food."

"What time?"

"Six."

"I'll be back."

As I left the room, Mom called after me, "You were wonderful, sweetheart."

The air was already hot when I reached the pool. The sun looked orange in the haze. I showed my pass at the gate and looked down from the deck to the main pool below. Half the team was already there, lying on towels in the grass. Kids from other grades were standing around, asking about the game. I laughed to myself. We'd beaten Ryewood. We were league champs.

Coach came through the gate with Lisa and Max.

"How does that elbow feel?" he asked, laying his arm around my shoulder.

"A little sore."

"A little? You give it a good rest. No pitching or lifting for a few days."

"Yes, sir!"

"You should have seen Danny pitch yesterday," he said to his wife. "Went the full nine innings."

"Congratulations," she said, her green eyes glittering in the warm morning light. "I heard it was a great game."

"The best," I replied.

Max began pulling his parents toward the pool.

"Coach?" I said.

He hung back a moment.

There were so many things I wanted to tell him. I wanted to thank him for spending so much time with me all year, for not losing faith in me when I was ready to quit, and for letting me finish the game yesterday. But the sun was hot and the water looked so inviting and Max was calling to him and Jim had just yelled, "Get down here, Koufax!" and the rest of the team was cheering, "Coach! Coach! Coach!" so all I said was "Thanks, Coach, for everything," then hurried down to the pool.

AUTHORS GUILD BACKINPRINT.COM EDITIONS are fiction and nonfiction works that were originally brought to the reading public by established United States publishers but have fallen out of print. The economics of traditional publishing methods force tens of thousands of works out of print each year, eventually claiming many, if not most, award-winning and one-time best-selling titles. With improvements in print-on-demand technology, authors and their estates, in cooperation with the Authors Guild, are making some of these works available again to readers in quality paperback editions. Authors Guild Backinprint.com Editions may be found at nearly all online bookstores and are also available from traditional booksellers. For further information or to purchase any Backinprint.com title please visit www.backinprint.com.

Except as noted on their copyright pages, Authors Guild Backinprint.com Editions are presented in their original form. Some authors have chosen to revise or update their works with new information. The Authors Guild is not the editor or publisher of these works and is not responsible for any of the content of these editions.

THE AUTHORS GUILD is the nation's largest society of published book authors. Since 1912 it has been the leading writers' advocate for fair compensation, effective copyright protection, and free expression. Further information is available at www.authorsguild.org.

Please direct inquiries about the Authors Guild and Backinprint.com Editions to the Authors Guild offices in New York City, or e-mail staff@backinprint.com.

Printed in the United States
6010